About the author

SHEENA WILKINSON has won many awards for short stories.

Her first novel, *Taking Flight*, won two Children's Books Ireland Bisto Awards, the most prestigious Irish awards for children's books. *Taking Flight* won both the Honour Award for Fiction and the Children's Choice Award, making Sheena one of only four writers ever to have received two awards in one year. It won a White Raven Award from the International Youth Library in Munich, and was chosen by IBBY (International Board on Books for Young People) as Ireland's representative in the writing category in their 2012 Honour List.

Grounded, the sequel, was one of *The Irish Times*' Children's Books of the Year and was shortlisted for the Children's Books Ireland Awards 2013. In November 2012, only two years after the publication of her first novel, Sheena was awarded a Major Individual Award by the Arts Council of Northern Ireland, which will allow her to take a year off her full-time teaching job to concentrate on writing.

Sheena lives in County Down with a lot of books, a timid cat and a naughty pony.

TOO MANY
PONIES

SHEENA WILKINSON

TOO MANY PONIES
Published 2013 by Little Island
7 Kenilworth Park
Dublin 6W, Ireland
www.littleisland.ie

ISBN 978-1-908195-25-8

British Library Cataloguing Data. A CIP catalogue record for this book
is available from the British Library.

Cover design by Pony and Trap
Typeset in 12-point Judson by Oldtown
Printed in Scotland by Bell & Bain Ltd.

Little Island receives financial assistance from
The Arts Council (An Chomhairle Ealaíon), Dublin, Ireland.

10 9 8 7 6 5 4 3

For

Elizabeth

Unlike Lucy, I was sensible enough to choose a wonderful friend at the very start of first year. Many years of friendship later, this is for her, with much love.

Chapter I

No Fun at Rosevale

ALL through her first morning at secondary school, Lucy wondered who the other horsey girls in her class were. Now, in form class, when they were all meant to Get to Know Each Other, she was going to find out.

'Think of your very favourite thing,' Miss Connor called, 'and find other people who love it too. Make a group. Talk!' She clapped her hands and beamed.

Thirty brand-new first years milled round muttering. Rugby players and Irish dancers and Justin Bieber fans searched for kindred spirits.

'Ponies!' Lucy shouted. 'Over here! Ponies!' She waved her arms around.

A girl with a banner of blond hair ran up, followed by some others. There was a lot of screaming and jumping up and down.

Lucy looked round the room. Most people were in a group, though some of the groups were just pairs. Aidan Kelly stood on his own by the door.

'Aidan!' Lucy called him over. 'Ponies! Over here.'

The room went quiet. Aidan didn't move.

'Aidan!' Lucy called again. 'Come on – you love ponies!'

'We don't want boys in our group,' the blond girl said.

'His dad owns the yard where I keep my pony,' Lucy said. 'He should definitely be in this group.'

'Come on – no stragglers!' Miss Connor called. 'Everybody must be interested in *something.*'

'Ooh, Aidan, you *love* ponies!' somebody from the rugby group said in a put-on squeaky voice.

The blond girl giggled. 'That's my twin,' she said.

Lucy saw the furious look Aidan gave her, but she didn't see which group he ended up in.

'Now,' said Miss Connor, 'let's see which group can find out most about each other. Off you go. Lots of questions.'

'Each person say the name of their pony and what colour it is and what it can do,' bossed the blond girl. She pointed to a small red-haired girl whose name, Lucy knew, was Erin. 'You first.'

'Oh, I haven't got a pony,' Erin said.

The blond girl widened her eyes as if Erin had said something outrageous like, *I haven't got a head.*

'So where do you ride?'

'Nowhere. We could never afford lessons.' Erin

said this with, Lucy thought, a slight challenge in her voice. 'But my granda says he's going to get me –'

The blond girl turned away. 'Oh well,' she said. 'I'll tell you about *my* pony. He's called Cody, and he –'

The bell blared and everybody went off to lunch. Lucy was going to wait for Aidan – he was pretty much her next-door neighbour and the only other person she knew from her primary school – but he shrugged her off with another of those angry looks. The blond girl was right, Lucy decided. They wouldn't bother with boys. Or with people who *claimed* to like ponies but couldn't even ride.

After lunch Lucy sat with the two other pony owners on a wall in the corner of the quad – she'd have to remember not to call it the playground – and went on talking about horses. The other two kept their ponies at the same yard and had been friends for ever. Jade's twin Josh didn't like ponies. Of *course* not. Like most boys, he thought ponies were stupid. 'There's no boys at *our* yard,' she said.

Lucy told them all about Puzzle. How he could jump a metre, easy. How when you gave him a treat, he held it in his lips and wouldn't eat it until you went away. How when you groomed his soft white belly he nipped you unless you remembered to dodge.

'And what are his colours?' Miranda, the other girl, asked.

Lucy stared at her. What a funny way of talking. Why not just *What colour is he?* And Lucy had already *told* them Puzzle was a piebald – that was how he'd got his name, because the patches of black and white were like jigsaw pieces.

'He's piebald,' she said again. 'Black and white,' she added, in case Miranda was a bit slow.

Jade rolled her dark blue eyes and Miranda giggled. 'His *colours*. Like, Sparkle's are pink and silver,' she explained. 'And Jade's just got new *everything* for her birthday for Cody, and it's all purple.' She ticked things off on her plump fingers. 'Purple numnah, purple travel rug, purple brushes, purple head-collar – *I* bought her that.'

Because I'm *Jade's friend, not you,* her eyes said.

'Ah.' Lucy understood now. She thought of her stable at Rosevale, with all her bits and pieces piled up outside, sometimes tidy, the way Declan, the owner, insisted on, but quite often not. Occasionally she couldn't even find her own stuff, but Aidan and his little sister Kitty never minded lending. And nobody cared what *colour* things were. They were too busy looking after the horses, ponies and donkeys. 'Too many ponies,' Declan kept saying. As if there could be such a thing as *too many ponies*.

'I have all different colours. Just whatever I can find.' Her voice trailed off a bit.

The other girls looked at her in disbelief.

'Oh, I don't think I'd like that,' Jade said.

'And purple really suits Cody,' Miranda said. 'Show Lucy that picture of him with everything on.'

They got out their phones and showed her pictures of their yard until the bell went for the end of lunch. None of the other ponies was a patch on Puzzle, of course, but they did look smarter. There was one photo of Miranda and Jade and a crowd of other girls on their ponies, all wearing matching jodhs and jackets. Not matching each other; matching their ponies' *colours.*

'And their yard sounds way more fun than Rosevale,' Lucy explained to her mum later when she picked her up from the school bus at the crossroads. Aidan had been on the bus too. She'd wanted to ask him why he'd pretended not to like ponies, but he'd been reading. 'They go to shows all the time. And Susie – that's who owns their yard – it's called Sunnyside Farm, isn't that a brilliant name? Anyway, Susie organises jumping competitions for them at the yard too, so they've all got heaps more rosettes than I have, *and*' – she paused dramatically to let the full weight of this sink in –'Susie let them paint their stable doors to match their ponies' colours. Like Jade's pony has everything purple, so his door is purple. And Miranda's pony has everything pink and silver, so –'

Lucy's mum shuddered. 'It sounds revolting.'

'Oh, Mu-um. You don't understand. They're all *friends*. They get to do everything together. There's loads of nice girls there. Susie doesn't let just anyone in. It's like a club. And *their* mums take them *everywhere*,' she added.

'In co-ordinating designer country casuals, no doubt,' Lucy's mum said, indicating right to turn into their road.

'Probably.'

'That reminds me – someone's bought Greenlands at last.'

'No!' Greenlands, about two miles up the road, a big old house with acres and acres of lush fields stretching uphill behind miles of stone wall, had been for sale as long as Lucy could remember, and as long as Lucy could remember she had fantasised about her parents buying it. Puzzle would have loved living on two hundred acres, and she could have had jumps everywhere. She sighed and fiddled with her seatbelt. 'Hurry up, Mum. I can't wait to ride Puzzle.'

'Homework?'

'Mostly covering books and things. I can do it after tea. You could let me off here,' Lucy suggested. 'To save time.'

From the corner, where the road made a sudden right-hand bend, with Rosevale's lane going uphill to the left, she could see Puzzle grazing under a tree with Aidan's old pony Midge, recently passed on to Kitty. The ponies were swishing their tails to keep the flies off each other.

'You are not going to the yard in your new uniform,' her mum said. 'It's only ten minutes' walk from the front door.'

Eight minutes, Lucy reckoned, timing herself as she walked up the hill to Rosevale a short while later, having changed into jeans and wellies. But she was probably faster than Mum. Having Rosevale next door was the main reason she was allowed a pony at all. So she could do her thing with Puzzle and not need lifts all the time. Lucy's parents were OK, but they didn't *get* ponies and they were always working.

The problem was that Rosevale wasn't a proper livery stable. Declan didn't mind keeping Puzzle, because they were neighbours, but really it was a sanctuary. Starving, abandoned, beaten or just plain neglected horses, ponies and donkeys were brought there from all over the country. An old lady called Doris had started it years ago, and left it to Declan and his wife Seaneen in her will. Only she hadn't left much money to look after it.

As she let herself in through the much-mended gate, Lucy stopped to watch Ned, the old donkey, who was supposed to be nearly forty, scratching his hairy grey flanks with his teeth. Rosevale looked scruffy in the September sun, its red corrugated iron roofs sagging and rusty. Behind the yard the house was old and grey, with millions of rooms, but freezing, Kitty had told her. All summer Declan had been saying he must get rid of the weeds along the drive, but all summer he had been too busy. Even with most of the horses out at grass, there were always some needing medical attention or being gently handled, to overcome their fear of people, or schooled, ready for re-homing. When Lucy had first come to Rosevale, she had hated to see the ponies moving on. But now she understood that these were the success stories. Once a pony was re-homed, it left space for another one. And Lucy's proudest moments were when Declan let her help by riding some of the ponies. She was stronger than Kitty and braver than Aidan.

Aidan worked hard in the yard – as hard as his dad, sometimes – but when Lucy asked him if he wanted to go out riding with her he usually said no. His new pony, Firefly, had been a show-jumper who fell on hard times after an injury and had been going for meat. He was fine now, but all Aidan seemed to do was hack him about the place like an old woman.

Aidan and Kitty were *OK*, Lucy thought, kicking a pebble up the drive and making a cloud of dust, but Aidan was a boy, and Kitty was too young. It wasn't

8

like having a crowd of girls to hang round with. A pony gang.

Aidan was in the yard when she reached it, washing what looked like a large pink dog but was in fact a tiny pink pony. At least, it wasn't exactly pink, it was grey, but its coat was so roughened and scabby and bare in places that its pink skin shone through, the effect enhanced by the pink surgical scrub that Aidan was using. It stood patiently, resting a hind leg, only flinching when Aidan touched a sore point. Its ribs stood out like a toast-rack.

I don't want to see ponies like that, Lucy thought. *I don't always want to be reminded of how cruel people are, and how animals suffer. I bet there aren't any scarecrows like that at Sunnyside Farm. I want to be on a yard that's fun.*

Then Aidan looked up from squeezing out his sponge and grinned. He was taller than Lucy, who was short and square, and he had dark eyes which, to her relief, were no longer blazing crossly at her the way they had at school.

'Hey, Lucy,' he said. 'Guess what? She took a carrot from me just now. First time she's trusted anyone enough. That's why I'm bathing her. She's not sure about it, but it'll make her feel better. Won't it, gorgeous?'

The ugly little pony's ears flicked at the sound of his low voice.

9

Lucy felt horrible. Of *course* she wanted to be at Rosevale. Of *course* she didn't want to be on a yard full of snobby girls with their colour-coded My Little Pony bling.

'Silly girls,' she told Puzzle half an hour later. His bouncy canter stride rocking-horsed them round the sand-school. '*We* don't care about things like that, do we?'

She ran her hand over her pony's black shoulder. (His other shoulder was white.) All the same, when she looked down at her faded brown numnah and her grubby saddle and her jeans and wellies – she wasn't absolutely sure where she'd left her riding boots – she thought she might smarten herself up a bit, now that she was in secondary school. Maybe Jade would invite her and Puzzle to ride at Sunnyside Farm – maybe even to go to a competition – and she wouldn't want to show herself up.

'Lucy?'

She looked over to the gate at the sound of Declan's low, firm tones. He never shouted – there were too many animals at Rosevale that freaked out at a raised human voice.

'Have you warmed him up properly?' He sat easily on Folly, his grey mare, who nobody else was allowed near because she was 'sensitive', Declan said. A nutter, Kitty said.

10

'Yes,' Lucy said, crossing her fingers.

She hadn't warmed up for *very* long. It had been a long day at school, all new subjects and keeping up with her new friends, and she'd been impatient to canter and jump, but it wouldn't do any harm. Puzzle had been mooching round the field all day with his mates. It wasn't as if he'd been stuck in a stable getting stiff.

Declan went on his way, Folly's hooves ringing on the concrete, and Alfie the grey lurcher's claws skittering beside them. Declan hacked round the fields every evening to check on all the animals. Lucy stood up in her stirrups to see if she could see Kitty or Aidan about to put up some jumps for her, but they were brushing the yard. After what she'd said to her new friends – and she might have exaggerated a tiny bit about how well Puzzle could jump – she wanted to make sure she kept practising.

'Why don't you come and jump when you've finished?' she yelled over.

'Don't shout,' Kitty said.

'We have to poo-pick the bottom paddock,' Aidan said. 'And Kitty has to muck out the foals.'

'No, *you* do,' argued Kitty.

Lucy gave up. It was all very well, rescuing ponies and being *good* all the time, but it didn't half make life boring for other people.

Chapter 2

Ponyboy

MR McCLUSKY gave out the novel they were going to read in English. *The Outsiders.* The blurb sounded OK, but Aidan hated being read to, unless the person was good and did all the voices. Mr McClusky had a voice like water going down a plughole.

Aidan zoned out and thought about September. She'd let him groom her yesterday, and for the first time he'd caught a glimpse of a pretty, snowy pony under the ribs and scabs. He called her September because she'd arrived on the first of September. Their dad always said not to name them, because they weren't going to be staying. But Aidan and Kitty could never resist naming the ponies, and sometimes they did have to stay.

September might have a chance of a new home, though. She was small and cute and willing to please. Even though humans had been horrible to her, she wanted to trust them. If Aidan had been September he'd have bitten and kicked.

He became aware of a giggle bubbling up round him.

'Ponyboy,' someone – Josh, he thought – said. 'No way, sir. Nobody can be called *Ponyboy*.'

'*Aidan* could,' said Olly, Josh's sidekick, in a thoughtful voice. 'He *loves* ponies.'

'Don't be silly, boys,' McClusky said. '"What's in a name? That which we call a rose by any other name would smell as sweet."'

Aidan flicked through the pages. The book was nothing to do with horses. The character was just called Ponyboy. Which, whatever McClusky said about roses, was totally stupid. Lucy turned round and grinned at him, but Aidan didn't smile back. If it hadn't been for Lucy, nobody here would ever have had to know that he liked horses.

They had PE in the afternoon. Aidan had liked PE at primary school – he was wiry and fit from working in the yard, and had been on the football team. Here they played rugby. Even so, he seemed to get the hang of it OK.

'Good effort,' said Holden, the coach, at the end of the session. 'We have rugby practice every Saturday morning – soon see how you shape up.'

'Sir – Saturday? I can't – I'm busy on Saturdays.'

Holden rolled back on the heel of his trainers so he could really look down his nose at Aidan. 'What could be more important than training for your school?

I don't invite just anyone to my Saturday sessions, you know.'

'I have to ... I help out at home.' He didn't want to mention the yard and the horses, with all the other boys listening, but as soon as the words were out he realised that it sounded like he spent his Saturdays hoovering or washing up or something.

Not even Olly or Josh laughed out loud, not with Holden looming, but Aidan knew they'd heard.

Queuing for the bus after PE, half-watching everybody jostling and carrying on, Aidan cheered himself up with the thought that in only half an hour he'd be walking up his own lane to his own chestnut pony, Firefly, and to poor scabby September. It was his turn to muck out the barn where the foals lived. It was a filthy job and he and Kitty fought to get out of it.

'Going home to do a bit of *helping*, Ponyboy?' Josh was so close that Aidan could smell his cheese-and-onion breath.

''Cause nasty wugby is for *boys*, isn't it?' Olly put on a high-pitched voice. '*I have to stay home and help my mummy.*'

'*I have to bwush my wittle pony's wuvly tail.*'

A couple of other boys giggled and pushed closer to see what the craic was.

Ignore them, Aidan thought, hating the sick churning of his stomach and the cold creeping of his skin. He stared at the ground. When you looked closely at concrete it wasn't just grey, the way you'd think. There were little splinters of colour in it.

Olly gave him a shove that propelled him into some older boys.

'Watch it,' they grumped.

The bus would be here in a minute. Aidan was right at the front of the queue. He'd make sure he got a seat at the front and he'd read his book again. If he ignored them they'd get bored. Everybody knew that.

'Oy, *Ponyboy.* I'm talking to you.'

'Well, don't,' Aidan said. 'I'm not talking to you.' But his voice squeaked thinly through a dry mouth and he wished he hadn't spoken.

'Ooooh, unfriendly!' Josh poked him in the chest – not hard, but enough to make him step back.

'Will you firsties wise up!' an older boy shouted.

Suddenly someone burst in and gave Josh a hard shove back. Someone short and square and cross.

'Leave him alone!' Lucy shouted. 'Pick on someone your own size.'

She stood poised, elbows ready to do more shoving if she needed to.

'Ooooh, here's your girlfriend,' Olly said.

'*I need my girlfwiend to save me fwom the nasty boys,*' Josh said.

The bus lumbered round the corner at that

exact moment and Aidan, at the front of the queue, stepped forward, away from the lot of them, feeling in his blazer pocket for his bus pass. *Half an hour,* he thought. *Half an hour until I'm home.*

And next day – well, next day, hopefully, they'd have moved on to someone else.

Chapter 3

Lucy's Brilliant Idea

PUZZLE cleared the cross-pole with a flick of his tail. *Too easy*, he seemed to say, as he gathered speed. Lucy steadied him for the corner and the big wall. It wasn't really a wall. Kitty and Lucy had piled boxes in front of an ordinary pole, but it was the solidest jump they had. Puzzle's black ears pricked and he soared over it.

'Again,' Lucy said, rubbing his shoulder. 'Come on, boy.' She had done the three jumps at least six times, and every time Puzzle had sailed over like a show-jumper.

'This is too easy for you, isn't it?' Lucy murmured. 'Bet the jumps at Sunnyside aren't like this. Bet *they've* got proper stripy poles and everything. And I bet there's always someone to help you put the jumps up.'

She felt a bit sore that she hadn't been invited to Sunnyside yet. The only place she'd been invited to was Erin's house, but when she told her mum where Erin lived – a big estate on the edge of Belfast – her mum said she couldn't go.

Lucy cantered round the sand-school, feeling Puzzle fit and fresh, ready to break into a gallop. *I want to go out for a ride*, his pounding hooves said. There were miles of tracks round the fields at Rosevale – that was one good thing – but they were only for walking and trotting. For most of the year the surface was too hard for speed, and anyway, Declan didn't like you disturbing the horses in the fields.

The sand-school gate swung open and Aidan appeared, leading a tiny grey. It took Lucy a moment to recognise it as the scabby pinkish pony.

'She looks better,' she called over, bringing Puzzle back to a walk. The pony's shoulders steamed. Lucy let him walk round on a long rein, and he stretched his neck out.

Aidan walked the little grey beside them. The ponies turned their heads towards each other with interest. Lucy tried not to stare at the grey's scabby coat. She hoped Puzzle couldn't catch anything from her.

'Aidan – have you told your dad about those boys?'

Aidan's face flushed. 'There's nothing to tell. And it's none of your business. I don't need you fighting my battles for me.'

'Well, you're not too good at fighting them yourself, are you?' Lucy kicked Puzzle into a trot and the grey flinched away at the sudden movement. When Lucy looked back over her shoulder, Aidan had his hands full calming her down. Lucy slowed Puzzle, feeling mean. 'Sorry,' she said. 'Didn't mean to scare her.'

Aidan sighed. 'It's OK. Just ... don't go on about *school*.'

From the way his face had gone, tight and closed, Lucy knew Aidan was serious. If anyone had been teasing her as much as Josh and Olly teased Aidan, she'd have hit them by now. Or at least *told*. But she changed the subject obediently: 'Do you think your dad would let us get new jumps?'

Aidan looked round at the greyish poles, dented barrels and old tyres. 'What's wrong with the ones we have?' he asked.

'Oh, Aidan, they're rubbish! Half the poles have been broken and there's no way of making anything more than a metre. Jade says –'

'*You* haven't jumped more than a metre!'

'Only because the jumps aren't big enough. I bet you I *could*.'

It was ages since she'd seen Aidan jump more than a *centimetre*. Firefly, who'd been a really good show-jumper in his day, was wasted on him.

'Well, you can always ask Dad,' Aidan said. 'There he is.'

Declan leaned over the gate. 'Going OK?' he asked Aidan.

'Declan,' Lucy said, bringing Puzzle to a halt by

the gate. 'Aidan and I were just saying, these jumps are a bit past it. I just wondered if there was any chance of some new ones?'

'Jumps?' Declan stared at her as if she had asked for the moon.

'Just a couple.'

Declan pushed his dark hair back from his forehead. 'Lucy, I'm turning horses away every day because I can't afford to feed them.' His voice was fierce. 'Bedding, shoeing, feed, hay, the vet – have you any idea how much the cost of everything has gone up in the past few years?

'Um... well...'

Lucy's parents were always complaining about this too, when they paid Puzzle's livery bill every month, but she didn't see what it had to do with a few proper jumps.

'So no – unless you buy them yourself, there is absolutely *no* chance of new jumps. And you're going to sicken that pony anyway.'

'Only because the jumps are so crap!'

She wished she had lots of money, but she was a terrible saver. They were meant to be having a big charity fund-raiser at school – the whole of the junior school. Maybe she could have a campaign of her own, for new jumps. Her mum might pay her to do chores.

'Dad,' Aidan said. 'There's plenty of old wood lying about. Could Lucy not take some of it and make some jumps?'

'Don't worry,' Lucy said, not wanting to give Declan the satisfaction of refusing. 'I'm sure you need all your spare wood for firewood or patching stables.'

'We do, actually,' Declan said. 'Aidan, the foals need to be mucked out.'

'It's Kitty's turn!'

'She's gone to visit your gran.'

Aidan sighed.

'I'll help,' Lucy offered. 'Soon as I cool Puzzle down.'

She looked thoughtfully at Declan's back as he walked away. He was always worried about money – Rosevale depended largely on donations – but she'd thought he was keen for Aidan to start jumping Firefly properly. So if he wouldn't even spare a bit of old wood – well, it meant things must be *really* tight.

The old barn was the most decrepit building at Rosevale. It was normally used for storing hay and shavings, but when Declan had been asked to take six tiny Welsh foals who'd been found tethered on some wasteland, he had patched up the roof and fenced off half the barn for them. It wasn't five-star accommodation, but they had a deep bed and plenty of hay. As always, at the sound of humans entering, the foals rushed to the bars of their improvised stall, pushing at Aidan and Lucy's hands.

'They're cheeky enough, anyway,' Lucy said, as a tiny chestnut with huge eyes chewed her sleeve. 'And they're getting big.'

'Dad says they're a nuisance,' Aidan replied.

'Aw, but they're so cute.' Lucy scratched the foal's fluffy brush of forelock. 'And they can't be much bother. It's not like you have six stables to muck out.'

'No. But we're kind of stuck with them. Nobody wants foals this young. OK, will you take this fork?'

Aidan barricaded the foals in a corner of their stall with a length of rope, and threw them some fresh hay to keep them occupied.

It was a dirty, sweaty job. The foals were mucked out every day, but they still managed to produce huge amounts of dung. Lucy dug her fork into a corner of the bed and it sank gloopily. Under her boots the bedding squelched.

'Ugh. Do you never take the wet out?' she asked. 'This is swimming.'

'Course we do.' Aidan flicked a forkful of dung onto the wheelbarrow. 'Every day.'

He set down his fork and came over to where Lucy's boots were sinking into the wet bed.

'Oh.' He frowned and dug the toe of his own boot in. 'Six foals can't have peed this much since last night.'

He lifted a handful of the darkened wet bedding and sniffed it.

'Eeww.' Lucy wrinkled her nose.

'It's just water.'

He looked up. Lucy looked up. The corrugated iron roof sagged above them, the way it always had. Except ...

'That bit of the roof has totally rusted through. No wonder the rain's got in.'

When you looked carefully you could see the grey of the sky in the gaps.

Aidan sighed. 'That's all we need. There's nowhere else for them and ... I'd better go and tell Dad.'

Lucy decided to stay where she was. She didn't want to see Declan's reaction. The foals, not knowing they were a nuisance, not caring that their home was falling down round them, kept on munching with their tiny mouths, their big eyes watching Lucy as she shovelled and dug and wondered how much a new roof would cost.

And that was when she had her first brilliant idea.

Chapter 4

Charity Case

MISS CONNOR clapped her hands in the way Aidan and the rest of 1C knew meant business.

'Now,' she said in her beamiest voice, 'who wants to nominate our special charity for this year?"

Several hands shot up – the people who'd actually spent the weekend thinking of a charity. Lucy waved hers around. Aidan never put his hand up in class, and anyway he hadn't thought of anything. He'd been too busy helping his dad to patch the barn roof and replace all the wet bedding. He'd hardly managed to finish his real homework, never mind extra thinking.

'Africa,' said someone.

'Africa's not a charity,' said Jade. 'It's a *country*.'

'It's a *continent*,' said Erin, who listened in class.

Jade gave Erin a mean, narrow-eyed stare that made her look just like her evil twin Josh. Aidan had no idea why Lucy was always hanging round that Jade. Even at the yard now, it was always *Jade says* ...

'Why don't I put down Oxfam?' suggested Miss Connor. Her eyes raked the room again. 'Oliver?'

'The rugby club,' Olly trumpeted.

There was an immediate outcry.

'It's not meant to be a *school* thing.'

'The rugby club's not a *charity*.'

Miss Connor banged on the board. 'It's got to be a proper charity,' she said. 'All right, Lucy, you don't need to wave your arm like that. I can see you perfectly well. Now, what's your idea?'

'Rosevale,' Lucy said promptly and grinned at Aidan.

For a moment he thought he hadn't heard her properly. Then, when Miss Connor said, 'And what sort of charity is that?' and Lucy started telling the class, he wished he could climb inside his schoolbag and never come out.

'It's a sanctuary for horses,' Lucy was saying in her clear voice. She actually stood up and everybody listened. 'They rescue them – often they're starving. Or they've been abused. Sometimes they've even just been abandoned – haven't they, Aidan?'

'Um,' said Aidan. He circled a scribble on his desk with his fingertip.

'*Aidan.*' Lucy's voice was cross. 'You can tell them better than me. It's *your* home.' When he didn't say anything, she went on in an even stronger voice.

'Aidan's dad runs it. But they could really do with the money. It costs a lot to look after horses. And they need to do some urgent repairs. And there's lots of horsey people in this class, so I think Rosevale is the charity we should support.'

She smiled round. Erin clapped.

'Thank you,' Lucy said and sat down.

'Well,' Miss Connor said, 'that was a lovely speech, Lucy. I'm sure we have lots of animal lovers in 1C. And it's good to support local charities.'

She wrote *Rosevale* on the board in her big loopy writing. It sat there in red board marker. Aidan kept his eyes fixed on his desk. Was Connor totally deaf? Could she not hear, above the general discussion about starving children and sick people and abused animals, what they were saying?

'Ponyboy lives in a sanctuary!'

'Yeah, a sanctuary for *losers.*'

'*Oh, my poor ickle pony.*'

'Any more ideas?' Miss Connor asked. 'Right, two minutes' discussion with your partner and then we'll vote.'

Aidan voted for Oxfam without lifting his eyes from his desk. Lots of the girls voted for Rosevale, but Oxfam won.

On the bus home Lucy sat with her chin in the air and wouldn't make eye contact, and when she came to ride Puzzle she didn't offer to help with anything.

'YOU'RE stupid,' Kitty said. She and Aidan were poo-picking in one of the fields – a boring job, but easy enough, apart from wheeling the full wheelbarrow to the muck heap afterwards. Firefly, Midge and Big Sam came over to poke their noses into the wheelbarrow and stayed around hoping for titbits, but then lost interest and started to graze. 'I'd love my class to raise money for here. It'd be cool.'

'Yeah, but ...' At the local primary school everyone knew Rosevale. Once, his dad had even brought old Ned into school and done a talk about cruelty to animals, and Aidan hadn't minded at all. Nobody had sat behind him singsonging *You live in a charity, you live in a charity.* 'Anyway,' he said, starting to push the wheelbarrow over to a heap of dung, 'it'll only be a cake sale or something. They'll probably raise hardly anything.'

'Hardly anything'd be better than nothing,' Kitty said. 'Dad said if feed prices go up again this winter he'd have to have some of the old horses put down.'

Aidan wheeled round so quickly that a dollop of dung flew off his fork and hit Kitty's wellie. He looked at Big Sam, dozing now by the hedge, his lower lip hanging.

'No way. Dad would never do that. You're just trying to make me feel guilty.'

27

Kitty shrugged. 'I heard him telling Mum. After the man came out to look at the barn roof. Come on – let's get this finished and go for a ride. While we still have ponies left.'

Chapter 5

Another Brilliant Idea

IT was Jade who told Lucy the amazing news.

'It's that lottery winner who bought Greenlands. Dermie Doyle.'

'Sounds like a spot cream.' Lucy still didn't like thinking of Greenlands belonging to anyone.

'Yes, but *listen*. Susie says he's some wee man from the back streets of Belfast, but he's desperate to get in with the horsey crowd, and this is how he thinks he'll do it: let us ride over his estate and give out – are you ready for this? – *five thousand pounds* to the best team. Susie says he's a joke, but his money's real enough. I wish you could be in *our* team, Lucy, but you all have to be from the same yard; it's the rules. If we win, Susie's getting a horse walker.'

Lucy knew Jade must have got it wrong – prizes at local horse shows were rugs and sacks of feed – not five thousand pounds. But when she looked online, she saw that Jade was right. She checked the rules, printed everything off and went to find Aidan. She ran him to ground in the library, colouring in the map they had to do for geography.

'What?' Aidan asked. He put his blue pencil back in the box and took out a green one.

Lucy handed the pages to him. He glanced at them, still colouring in.

'So?'

'We could win five thousand pounds for Rosevale!'

'What do you mean *we*?'

Lucy jabbed a finger at the print-out. 'It has to be teams from yards. Four in a team. It can be a mix of adults and kids. There's big jumps and wee jumps beside each other and it's up to you which you pick. You can mix and match. There's more points for the big ones.' Lucy hoped she and Puzzle would be able to do the big jumps. She wasn't so sure about Aidan. 'Anyway, I've worked it out. The Rosevale team can be your dad, me, you and Kitty. I mean, you'll need to practise your jumping, but Firefly could do it OK.'

'Dad'll say there isn't time.'

'Aidan, it's for *five thousand pounds*. Think what that could do at Rosevale! You could get a whole new barn, never mind patching up the roof! You could buy hay for the whole winter. You could –'

'We wouldn't have a chance.'

Aidan went back to colouring in his stupid map.

He'd mixed up Belarus and Ukraine, but Lucy wasn't going to tell him.

She flounced. 'You're pathetic, Aidan Kelly! Well, I've texted Kitty and *she's* up for it. And if you aren't, we'll get someone else.'

Though she didn't know who. If only Rosevale were a normal yard, with lots of competitive teenagers. Like Sunnyside. Still, Declan was a brilliant rider – in his teens he had won some big competitions on a horse called Flight. And Kitty was as good as Lucy. Aidan would be the weak link – she hadn't seen him jump for ages – but the three of them would be so good they'd make up for it.

The competition was at Hallowe'en. That gave them about six weeks. Was that long enough to get the horses fit and trained? It would have to be. In her imagination Lucy and Puzzle soared over solid timber fences, and below them a crowd roared and clapped. She saw the cheque for five thousand pounds. She saw a brand new barn, hay piled to the roof, enough for ten winters.

And surely there might be enough left over for a few new jumps.

Somewhere in the middle of the dream she saw Jade and Miranda looking on with envy as the lottery winner put the winner's sash over Puzzle's head.

Declan would have to say yes.

Chapter 6

It's Only Jumping

AIDAN didn't think for a moment that his dad would agree. The chances of winning were so remote. But Kitty got home from school first. And by the time Aidan saw his dad she'd obviously got round him.

'Sure, it'll be a day out,' he said. He was filling hay-nets in the barn. Automatically Aidan started helping. 'I saw Cam at the feed shop,' his dad went on. Cam ran a small riding stables about six miles away. She had been his dad's first boss and was still one of his best friends. 'Seemingly everybody's talking about it. It's ridiculous – five thousand pounds! But if this Dermie Doyle wants the horsey crowd galloping all over his land then he's going to have it. Though Cam can't enter – not enough people are keen at her yard.'

There aren't enough people keen at *this* yard, Aidan thought. 'But you always say we haven't time for that kind of thing.'

His dad sighed and tightened the string on the net he had just filled. 'I know. But your mum's always saying you and Kitty have all work and no play with the horses. You'd enjoy it, wouldn't you? And Firefly's a great jumper.'

Aidan bit his lip and pushed hay down into the net. He knew *Firefly* could do it – it was himself he wasn't so sure of. And cross-country – those big solid fences. It had been different when Midge was his pony. He'd grown up on Midge.

'I don't mind the work,' he said.

'You can have a practice tonight,' his dad said, straightening up. 'Just in the school.' He made it sound like it wasn't a big deal at all.

While Aidan brought the ponies in, Kitty and Lucy set up a course in the sand-school. The jumps looked huge. When Firefly saw them he pranced and pulled.

'Steady, boy,' Aidan said, and ran his hand over Firefly's neck. His pony flicked his red ears as if he remembered his show-jumping past.

'Ah, look at Firefly. He can't wait,' Kitty said to Lucy.

Lucy played with Puzzle's thick mane. 'Thought your dad was meant to be coming?'

'He's had to go and fix one of the fences in the far field. But he'll be here as soon as he can.'

Maybe, Aidan thought, *if it's only the girls watching me, not Dad, it won't be so bad.*

'OK. Pretend it's a competition,' Kitty bossed. 'Down the long side, over the bales, then round and –'

'We have to warm up first.' Aidan spoke for the first time. 'You can't just start jumping.'

'I meant *after* we'd warmed up. I'm not stupid.'

They rode round the sand-school a few times on each rein, walking and trotting. It was ages since Firefly had been in the school – usually Aidan hacked him round the tracks between the fields. He liked seeing the horses grazing, and checking up on the fences. He liked riding when there was a *point* to it, when you *went* somewhere. Not this going round in circles and then –

It's only jumping, he told himself firmly.

Lucy headed off on Puzzle. Aidan thought the first two jumps were at a funny angle but Puzzle didn't have any bother. He cleared everything with a swish of his tail. Lucy sat balanced and relaxed, moving with her pony, making it look easy. Aidan's stomach knotted exactly the way it did when he looked out of the bus window and saw Olly and Josh at the bus stop.

Stupid, he told himself. *A few wee jumps in your own school. All you have to do is hold on and steer.*

Kitty went next. She went too fast into the wall and there was a nasty moment when Midge checked and it looked like he might refuse, but Aidan knew Midge never refused. Kitty was left behind, but she landed safely, laughing.

'You pushed on too much there. Lucky for you your pony knows how to get out of trouble,' said his dad's voice. He'd just arrived, and sat on Folly with Alfie beside them as usual, watching everything with doggy interest from under his shaggy grey fringe. Folly snatched at her bit, goggled with her big black eyes, and ran backwards, her front legs scrabbling and half-rearing above the ground. Aidan's dad hardly moved in the saddle. Aidan wouldn't have sat on Folly for a million pounds.

'Who's next? Aidan?'

Aidan shortened his stirrups, checked his girth, trotted Firefly in a circle. The jumps lurked like monsters, mocking him. Firefly tossed his head impatiently. He felt like a raging charger instead of a fourteen-hand pony.

'Get on with it, Aidan,' his dad said, and Kitty made a noise like a bell ringing.

The first jump wasn't so bad. Firefly was over-keen and jumped big, so that Aidan was pushed right up onto Firefly's neck and landed with a bump in the saddle that must have hurt the horse, but before he had time to worry they were cantering towards the next one, the one Lucy and Kitty insisted on calling 'the wall'. *It's only a few old boxes*, Aidan told himself, his heart pounding. *Even if we hit them we won't do any damage. Except maybe to the boxes.*

But everybody's watching. Your sister. Your dad. A girl out of your class. What's the big deal, Ponyboy?

His hands jerked at the reins and Firefly didn't know what he was asking.

'For God's sake, *steer*, Aidan!'

At the last minute Firefly swerved and Aidan shot halfway out of the saddle. He lost his stirrups but somehow managed to slither back and regain control. Firefly huffed and danced a bit. Aidan had to walk him round the sand-school before he settled again.

'Aidan!' his dad said. 'That was totally your fault! The pony needs you to tell him what to do. *You're* in charge.'

No I'm not, thought Aidan, as, at the insistence of his dad and under the impatient glares of the girls, he went round again and, this time, managed to clear the jump. *I'm not in charge of Firefly. I'm not in charge of whether I want to be in their stupid team or not. I'm not in charge of anything.*

Chapter 7

The Weakest Link

'CAN I be your partner?' Erin asked as 1C filed into the computer room.

Lucy was about to say yes when Jade made a beeline for her.

'*I'm* working with Lucy,' she said.

'I think Lucy can speak for herself,' Erin said.

'Um, well,' Lucy said, 'Miranda's at the orthodontist so ...'

Erin turned away. Lucy sat down beside Jade and logged on. They were in form class, making posters for their charity event – a cake sale and car wash.

'So how's *your* cross-country team coming on?' Jade asked.

'Great,' Lucy said. She highlighted the title and changed it to a wacky font.

'That looks awful,' Jade said and changed it back again.

Lucy didn't mind. She wasn't very artistic. The only

good thing about making these posters was that you were allowed to chat.

'You should see Folly – that's Aidan's dad's horse,' she went on. 'She's about sixteen now, but she's a brilliant jumper. But then Declan's won at Balmoral and everything.'

She didn't add that this had been before Aidan was born.

She didn't add that they hadn't even done any cross-country jumps yet, that they couldn't because they didn't have any.

She didn't add – partly because she didn't want to think about it, but also because it would have been mean, especially with him sitting two rows behind, working with Erin as they had both been the odd ones out – that Aidan was definitely the weak link in their team. Which put a lot of pressure on Lucy and Declan to clear the bigger jumps. Kitty, though she was a tight rider and brave, was only nine, and her pony only twelve-two.

She didn't ask Jade how the Sunnyside team was getting on because she'd been hearing about it every day – the flatwork lessons in the indoor school, the weekend practices over the purpose-built cross-country jumps, the special competition diet for the ponies and the brand-new matching purple tops with Sunnyside Farm embroidered on them.

'We're going up to Cam Brooke's yard tonight,' Lucy said. 'To practise round her cross-country jumps.'

'Why?' Jade asked. 'Do you not even have your own cross-country course at Rosevale?' She changed the lettering to blue.

'Um,' said Lucy. 'Just for a change.'

But Jade had lost interest and wanted to talk about her birthday instead. 'Josh and I always have a joint party,' she said, 'so I don't know how many people I'm allowed to invite. I mean I want to invite *you*, of course. But not *everyone*.' She made her eyes big and spoke in a loud, obvious whisper, which Lucy felt was meant for Erin.

'Jade and Lucy, less chat, more work,' called out Miss Connor.

'It's this cross-country competition, miss,' Jade said. She flashed Miss Connor the wide smile that teachers loved. 'We're just so excited.' She gave her shoulders a little wriggle.

'Yeah, we can't wait, miss,' Olly said unexpectedly from his seat beside Josh.

'I wouldn't have put you down as an equestrian enthusiast, Oliver,' Miss Connor said.

'Well, *I* have to support my twin, of course,' Josh replied.

'And *I* have to support my mate,' Olly added, and they high-fived.

'Isn't that lovely,' Miss Connor said.

Olly turned round to Aidan. 'We really can't wait to see *you* perform, Ponyboy,' he said. And smiled.

IN Cam's yard the ponies came off the lorry calmly, unlike Folly, who had sweated up during the short journey and barged off the ramp with her head in the air, neighing shrilly. Alfie slunk behind Declan. Lucy, Aidan and Kitty led their ponies round a bit. They looked about them with interest, and Midge nickered loudly.

'Steady, you silly old sausage.' Cam came forward to give Declan a hand with Folly. She looked at the ponies. 'Looking fit,' she said. 'Get tacked up and we'll head out. I'm coming too. Got a youngster who needs the experience. Ex-racer. Probably have kittens when he sees he's going out in a crowd.'

Lucy had met Cam a few times – she came to Rosevale now and again – but this was the first time she'd been to her yard. It was old-fashioned, like Rosevale, but very spruce and painted. A girl was brushing the yard, and horses and ponies looked out from over their half doors, pausing in their hay-munching to check out these strangers. Declan had started his career here, working at weekends since he was sixteen and then full-time before he took over Rosevale. Cam was about the same age as Lucy's mum, with short, greying red hair.

'See you in a minute,' she called over her shoulder. Declan, busy calming Folly down, didn't reply.

'Midge came from here,' Kitty said. 'Cam gave him to Dad when Aidan was born, only he's mine now.'

'Only till you outgrow him,' Aidan said quickly. 'Then he becomes mine again.'

He sat on Firefly, looking perfectly at ease. At ordinary riding, Lucy had to admit, he was as good as Kitty – maybe better because Kitty could be a bit rough and ready. It was only when they jumped that he turned into such a wuss.

'Yeah, what are *you* going to do with a twelve-two,' Kitty asked, 'when we've got too many ponies anyway?'

By the time they were all tacked up Cam had come back, mounted on a long-legged bay thoroughbred, which neighed at the new arrivals.

They followed Cam out of the yard, twenty hooves making a great clatter on the path. Lucy went at the back and watched the rest of her team critically as they crossed the road and went through the gate into the farm trail on the other side of the road. She imagined them riding up to the start of the cross-country course at Greenlands. If she didn't know them, how would she rate them as a team?

Folly jogged and snatched at her bit, her silvery mane floating in the breeze. She was, as Lucy had

41

told Jade, a brilliant jumper, but she needed a lot of jollying along. Midge bustled along, reliable but small. Firefly, at least on paper, was probably the best of the three, though Lucy felt bad thinking that when she was riding Puzzle. Firefly was an elegant, leggy pony whose bright chestnut coat gleamed in the autumn sunshine, the same colour as the leaves that were just starting to fall. He had powerful hindquarters and a long, raking stride. Unfortunately, as they got closer to the jumps set out at intervals in the fields, Aidan was starting to look tense and the pony was picking up on it. Lucy could tell from the way Firefly tossed his head and arched his neck that he was becoming unhappy. She pushed Puzzle on to catch up.

'Relax,' she said.

Aidan frowned at her. 'I'm perfectly relaxed,' he said through gritted teeth.

Lucy decided to catch up with Cam instead.

Cam smiled at her over her shoulder. 'Just watch his back end,' she warned. 'I don't *think* he kicks.'

'He doesn't look like he's going to kick,' Lucy said, but she kept a good distance from the bay thoroughbred's back legs as she brought Puzzle alongside him.

Cam halted her horse, Tyrone, at the entrance to a big field, and called out, 'OK, this is probably the best place to start. You can see the jumps. Most of them are only logs, nothing to worry about. We'll canter round the field and let the horses see the lie of the land and then take the jumps in turn.' She surveyed the team critically. 'Who's going to lead?' she asked. 'No point asking my eejit.'

'I'll lead,' Declan suggested.

Folly pawed the ground and put her ears back at Tyrone, who backed away in terror.

Cam widened her eyes. 'Are you kidding?' she said.

'Well, maybe not.' It was funny to see Declan being bossed around for a change. Next minute Lucy's heart danced when Declan said, 'Lucy can lead. Her pony's a hundred per cent. He won't stop.'

'Fine.' Cam smiled at Lucy. 'Take your time. You'll find the ground a bit soft at that first log – but don't let that put you off. The others are fine. Only do the downhill *if* you feel ready for it – that goes for all of you. I'll keep an eye out here to make sure everybody gets home safely. Which you all will,' she said quickly to Aidan, who hadn't uttered a word since the jumps had come into sight.

Lucy nodded and they all set off in a line round the outside of the big field – first trotting, then, at Cam's order, breaking into a canter. Puzzle gave a snort of pleasure and lunged into a fast, ground-eating gallop.

'Steady!' Cam called.

Lucy sat down and steadied Puzzle, and he settled

43

into a lovely rocking canter. Lucy felt her face break into a huge grin. This was wonderful, feeling her pony keen but obedient, sensing his eagerness to tackle the half-dozen jumps set in a trail round the field, hearing the hoof-beats of the others behind her and seeing nothing ahead but the short grass and the welcoming jumps.

She turned Puzzle into the first jump – a small log. The take-off was muddy, as Cam had said, but Puzzle never minded getting his hooves wet. He popped over it in a business-like manner and they were soon cantering up the hill to the next one, which wasn't much higher but had quite a spread. She felt Puzzle reach and stretch and land confidently.

'Good boy,' she breathed, looking for the next jump. She was aware of the others behind, but only dimly. The world had shrunk to her and her pony and the wonderful jumps.

We can do it, she thought, sitting back slightly as they headed down the hill again. Lucy hadn't much experience jumping downhill, but Puzzle cantered on steadily and she knew he wouldn't refuse. The jump flew at them, sooner than she expected. For a terrible moment she thought she was going to get left behind, but she let the reins slip through her fingers to avoid jagging Puzzle in the mouth, and, through a mixture of luck, timing and balance, managed to get back in the saddle in time to steer him for the last jump, another easy log.

After that, ignoring what Cam had said, she gave Puzzle his head and let him gallop towards the gateway where Cam was waiting. Tyrone backed off in alarm as she pulled Puzzle to a shuddery halt.

'Sorry,' she panted. 'I couldn't resist.'

'Well, remember cross-country isn't all about galloping,' Cam said. But she was smiling. 'You've a good pony there. Has he done much?'

Lucy glowed and patted Puzzle's sweating neck. 'He did more with his first owner,' she said. 'But we don't have our own transport and Rosevale ... Well, there isn't much time for shows and things.'

Cam nodded but Lucy saw that she wasn't really paying attention – she was looking with narrowed eyes up the hill to where the others were jumping. Lucy followed her gaze.

Folly flew over the downhill like a champion, Declan hardly moving in the saddle.

Kitty cantered past the downhill, but took the final jump beautifully.

'I'm going to try the downhill now,' she yelled over. 'I just wanted to see it close up!'

'OK!' Cam yelled back, making Tyrone twitch his long bay ears. 'Sorry, Ty. You're seeing a bit of life tonight, aren't you? Now, where's Aidan? Oh, there

45

he is. Gosh, he won't clear the downhill going like that. He shouldn't try it. He's not ready.'

It was just like in the school the other night. Aidan approached the jump looking as if he really didn't want to do it, his body braced and his hands pulling at the reins, first one way then the other, so that Firefly – who could have jumped it in his sleep – veered to the side, hesitated, then dropped a shoulder and ran out. Aidan sailed over his shoulder and landed in a heap.

Spooked by the wide open space, Firefly galloped back up the hill, reins and stirrups flying, then stopped at the top, looked round him, neighed loudly at his friends and cantered over to Lucy and Cam. It was an easy matter for Lucy to jump off Puzzle and catch him.

'Whoa,' she said, patting his neck. She turned round to see Cam riding across to the jump and the heap of Aidan lying in the grass. *Get up,* Lucy thought. She wanted to go and see what was happening, but with a pony's reins in each hand, she was pretty much stuck there. The best she could do was to let both ponies graze while she watched.

Cam, Declan and Kitty had all ridden over to Aidan, and Declan had dismounted and was kneeling beside him.

It hadn't *looked* like a bad fall; Lucy had come off that way herself millions of times, and often with a harder landing than the soft turf of Cam's cross-country course. Even so, Aidan didn't seem to be moving. Lucy's insides began to curdle. Aidan wasn't much good on the team but he was all they had. You weren't allowed to enter with three. If he'd broken his leg or something...

And it wasn't just about the money now – though of course she wanted to help Rosevale – it was the jumping itself, the thrill of hurtling cross-country with her own brave, clever pony. Was this the end of their chances?

No, of course not. Aidan was getting up now, flicking mud off himself, looking round for Firefly, talking to his dad. He was fine. Cam pointed down the field to where Lucy was standing with the two ponies. Lucy waved, and Aidan walked down the field to her. He held out his hands for Firefly's reins.

'Thanks for catching him,' he said briefly.

'Are you OK?'

'Yep.'

Aidan held Firefly's reins, put his foot in the stirrup and sprang up. Landed in the saddle, he stroked Firefly's chestnut neck. He didn't seem in a rush to go anywhere.

'Cam said *only* do the downhill if you felt ready,' Lucy reminded him. 'Maybe you just weren't ready.'

Aidan swung Firefly round and rode back to the others without replying.

Well! There was no need to be so rude. Lucy was only trying to be helpful. She followed at a distance, not wanting to miss anything.

'The important thing is to try again,' Cam was saying as Lucy and Puzzle approached. 'Don't worry about the downhill – just go and do the first wee log again – you had no problem with that, did you?'

Aidan shook his head, but made no move towards the jump.

'I'll give you a lead,' Kitty said. 'Firefly loves Midge – he'd follow him anywhere, never mind over a tiny wee log like that.'

'No, *I'll* give you a lead,' Declan said.

'And I'll keep an eye on you,' Cam said. 'Just relax. Take it really steady.'

Lucy didn't say anything in case she got her head bitten off again.

'You and Kitty stay here,' Cam ordered. 'Walk your ponies round on a loose rein. We'll call it a night once we've got Aidan over this jump.'

'They don't want us interfering,' Kitty complained, as she and Lucy obediently rode round the bottom of the big field. 'Firefly'd follow Midge way better than Folly. Dad just likes being the boss.' She wriggled her shoulders. 'I don't know why Aidan's so feeble. *I* did it, and Midge is only twelve-two.'

Aidan could have done it on Midge too, Lucy

thought, but she didn't say it. She played with Puzzle's mane and looked up the field. Folly trotted up to the jump, only cantering the last few strides, and popped over it without any fuss. Behind her, Firefly trotted, swerved and ran out to the side. Aidan didn't fall off this time, but he lost a stirrup and had to gather himself together.

Kitty looked at Lucy in despair. 'Firefly can *do* this,' she wailed. 'And Aidan never used to be so rubbish. He used to jump all the time in the school.'

'Maybe it's because it's cross-country?'

Kitty shrugged. 'He's such a cowardy custard. And he's got so grumpy since he went to big school. Mum has to drag him out of bed every day.'

Lucy hesitated. She had a pretty good idea why. Olly and Josh never missed the chance to get a dig at Aidan and he didn't seem to have made friends like she had. Should she tell Kitty? But she remembered how cross Aidan had been when she mentioned it, and how he'd told her not to fight his battles for him. OK, then, she wouldn't.

But she hoped, for the sake of the team, for the sake of Rosevale, that he'd start winning the battle he was having with jumping.

Cam's clear voice drifted down to them.

'OK. Stop making such a big thing of it. Relax. Breathe! It's meant to be fun.'

From where Lucy and Kitty were standing, having given up the pretence of walking their ponies round, it didn't look much like fun. Again Folly popped over the log. Again Firefly ran out at the last minute.

'Aidan! You have to approach it like you mean it! You're making the pony think there's something to be afraid of – some reason not to jump.'

A third time, the same thing, and then Aidan's voice, 'I can't do it! I told you I couldn't do it.'

And Declan, sounding like he was at the very edge of patience: 'Of course you can do it. It's only a wee log. You were doing much bigger than this in the school.'

'I *can't.*'

Aidan kicked his feet out of his stirrups and jumped off.

'You can't leave it like that! Do you want him to think he can refuse any time he feels like it?'

'I don't care, because I'm not doing it.'

Lucy had never heard Aidan sound so fierce. She looked at Kitty whose round cheeks were bright red under their smattering of freckles.

'I could kill him,' Kitty said. 'He's disgracing our whole family. Our whole yard.'

'Our whole team,' agreed Lucy.

Above them, Cam was walking over towards Aidan. She took hold of Firefly's reins. It looked like she was talking to Aidan but, annoyingly, too quietly for Lucy to hear. Then she raised her voice and called Lucy over.

Lucy looked at Kitty and shrugged, and rode over to the small group. Cam looked hassled, Declan furious and Aidan's face was scarlet. Lucy didn't know if he was angry or – as she would have been – mortified.

'Lucy,' Cam said. 'We can't let Firefly get away with running out, and Aidan's a bit ... upset ... after his fall. Would you pop him over it, please? Just once and then we'll call it a night.' She sounded as if she couldn't wait to get rid of them.

'OK.' Lucy jumped off Puzzle and handed his reins to Cam. Tyrone backed away nervously, then decided Puzzle wasn't a monster and they snuffed noses in a friendly way. Aidan handed Lucy Firefly's reins without a word. She opened her mouth to say she was sorry; she was only obeying Cam. Aidan must understand that he couldn't leave things like that, but Aidan's eyes were so hard and dark and angry that she only said, 'I'll just shorten the stirrups.'

Firefly felt funny after Puzzle. He was taller, his shoulders in front of the saddle were narrower and, right now, darkened with sweat. His long red ears flicked backwards and forwards, showing his uncertainty.

Lucy spoke to him softly. She could sense the pony was confused and worked up, but gradually, as she walked him round on a loose rein, then gathered him together for a steady trot, she felt him relax. She pushed him into canter and he responded with a low, long stride, very different from Puzzle's bouncy one. She turned him into the jump, felt him hesitate, but she was ready, steering him firmly and using her legs but, most importantly, she thought, *willing* them over, trying to remind him that jumping was fun.

Firefly cleared the jump beautifully.

'Good boy,' Lucy said, patting him.

As they cantered on up the slope, she thought she might as well go over the downhill too – after all that was the jump that had started the trouble in the first place. If Aidan saw that Firefly could do it, it might give him confidence.

Lucy turned Firefly at the top of the hill and trotted down. She cantered the last few strides, felt Firefly gather himself, and then they were over and cantering back to the others.

Lucy felt the grin split her face. That had been brilliant! Jumping Puzzle was wonderful because Puzzle was her own pony and a great jumper, but getting on a strange pony that was upset and had lost confidence, and getting the best out of him – that was even better.

She had forgotten Aidan. It was only when he held his hands out for the reins that Lucy thought how annoying it must be to see someone else ride your own pony better than you.

'Hope you didn't mind me doing the downhill,' she said, sliding her feet out of the stirrups. 'But he felt so good and I knew he could do it. It's just confidence.'

They rode back to the yard in silence, a slight drizzle misting the ponies' manes. And this time Lucy didn't find it so easy to imagine them riding together at the Greenlands competition as a team.

Chapter 8

Quitting

AIDAN stared at his cornflakes and his stomach churned. He ached all over from the fall last night.

'The jumps were *weeny*,' Kitty said for the hundredth time. 'Firefly probably couldn't even *see* them.'

'Leave him alone, Kitty,' his mum said, pouring milk into her tea. 'Not everybody's good at the same things.'

'But you *can* jump!' Kitty said. 'You used to jump. You're just out of practice.' She banged her spoon in frustration. 'You *have* to do it. There's nobody else.'

Aidan's dad came in from the yard, told Alfie to go to his basket and came to the table. He gave Aidan's mum a quick hug, then poured himself a cup of tea.

'Is it just nerves, Aidan?' he asked. 'Do you want me to give you a few lessons?'

That was the last thing he wanted. His dad was a terrible teacher. Because it came so easily to him, he had no idea how to teach anybody else. Aidan and Kitty had grown up riding ponies, but every so often

Dad decided their style was terrible and would make them trot for hours without stirrups.

'Dad,' Kitty said. 'What are we going to wear? We need to match. Can we get tops with "Rosevale" on them?'

'No,' said Dad.

'We are still going to *do* it, aren't we?' Kitty's voice was desperate.

'Kitty, give it a rest.'

Aidan bent over his bowl and pushed bits of cornflake around. Again he relived that horrific sense of tearing downhill out of control, Firefly ignoring him. The swerve. The ground slamming into him, knocking his breath out.

And far worse than that, everybody watching while he got it wrong again and again. And Lucy, blasted Lucy, making it look easy. *It's just confidence.* Like he didn't *know* that. Like it was that simple.

'Eat your breakfast, Aidan,' Mum said.

'I'm not hungry. I feel sick.' That was becoming truer by the minute.

'He's sulking,' Kitty said.

'Kitty. Leave your brother alone.' His dad's voice was fierce.

Aidan forced some cornflakes into his mouth, tried to swallow, then made a sudden dash to the downstairs loo and threw up.

55

'Aidan!' His mum stood at the door, her mouth a worried O. 'You didn't hit your head when you fell off, did you?'

He shook his head, shivering and wretched. 'I'm not doing it,' he shouted. 'I told you. I told them. I AM NOT DOING IT.' He heard his voice rising to a scream through a throat swollen with tears and stinging with puke. He felt extremely strange. Not exactly sick any more, but as if he was going to explode.

'Aidan! You don't *have* to do it. Not if it's upsetting you this much. Come on, it's OK.' She tried to hug him, but he cringed away. Dad and Kitty hovered round the door looking worried (Dad) and furious (Kitty).

'Bed,' Mum said. 'You can't go to school in this state. Kitty, you're going to be late.'

Aidan trailed back to his room, pulled off his uniform and got into bed, curling up with the hot-water bottle his mum brought him, and Bernard, the nicest of their three cats. He heard, as if in a dream, Alfie barking, Kitty whingeing and the foals kicking from the barn. At ten past eight, the time he normally got on the school bus, his whole body relaxed. When his mum came to check on him he squeezed his eyes shut and made his breathing slow. He heard her talking to his dad outside the door.

'I should stay off work and look after him,' his mum said, 'but we can't afford –'

'No, it's OK. I'm here. I'll talk to him later. It's just a reaction to all this jumping business. He takes things so seriously. Och, Seaneen, I wish he wasn't so ...'

Aidan pulled the duvet over his head.

At ten o'clock, with his mum safely at work and his dad out in the yard, he went down to the kitchen and made himself a huge pile of toast and a mug of tea. If he stocked up on food in secret, he might be able to convince them he was actually sick, and stay off school for ages. No Olly and Josh; no *Ponyboy*.

Except he couldn't stay away from Kitty and Lucy and his dad and the shaming memory of being so useless. And they knew he wasn't sick, really.

I wish he wasn't so ...

I know! Aidan thought. *I wish I wasn't so ... either!*

Through the window he saw the yard filled with sunshine. The horsebox was gone. He remembered that his dad was taking the skewbald cob to a new home. She was permanently lame, but she was going to be a companion for someone's pony.

Aidan went outside. The foals kicked their partition when they heard him, and from the paddock beside the drive Ned brayed long and loud. Ned had been ancient even in Doris Rose's time. What if Dad decided his time had come now? He wandered down to the bottom field. Firefly was grazing by the gate. Aidan scratched him in the place he liked, halfway up his neck, and Firefly snorted horsey slobber all over Aidan and looked angelic. 'You weren't so good last night,' Aidan told him, but he knew it wasn't Firefly's fault.

He might as well clean out the foals. They were in a different corner of the barn now, without quite as much room, and everybody was praying there wouldn't be too much rain before they got the roof fixed properly. Aidan's dad had patched it up in the meantime, but the roof was more patch now than anything else.

It was such a lovely day that he decided to let the foals out into the school for a play around. He led them out three at a time, and they danced round him and chewed their lead ropes. In the school they romped and kicked out their back legs and gawked with disbelief at the jumps.

He had the barn mucked out, September groomed and the yard brushed when his dad drove in.

'You've made a miraculous recovery,' he said.

Aidan shrugged. He and his dad lifted sacks of feed into the barn.

'Aidan?' his dad said without looking at him. 'Did you mean it? About the team?'

He bit his lip. He could say no, he hadn't meant it, but he knew that would just land him back where he was last night.

'Yeah,' he said. 'I meant it. I'm not jumping.'

'That's OK,' his dad said. 'It doesn't matter.'

But Aidan knew he didn't mean it.

Chapter 9

A Change of Team

LUCY's mind wouldn't take in what Kitty was trying to tell her.

'But ... but he can't *quit*! He can't let us all down like that! Look, we'll go and tell him, you and me. Tell him he *has* to do it.'

She strode down the yard as if she was going to haul Aidan out from wherever he was skulking. He'd been off school yesterday, but today he'd been in class with her all day and hadn't had the guts to tell her. Letting a nine-year-old do his dirty work. When she found him she'd ...

Kitty caught her up and grabbed her arm. 'No,' she said. Her eyelids were swollen and pink. Lucy had *never* seen Kitty cry, except when animals died. 'D'you think I haven't tried? But he just goes all weird. And now Mum says we're not allowed to even *mention* it.'

Lucy wanted to scream and stamp. 'But it's stupid.'

'I suppose he can't help not being as good as us.' Kitty gave a loud sniff.

'Lucy! Kitty!'

It was Seaneen, Kitty's mum. She wasn't in the yard much, but now she flew out of the barn holding a dandy brush and giving them death looks. 'You are *not* to talk about your brother like that,' she said fiercely.

Kitty burst into noisy tears and fled round the side of the barn. Seaneen raised her eyes to the sky and went back inside. Lucy went after Kitty.

'It's OK for you!' Kitty said between sobs. 'You don't live here. You don't really care. We won't be able to take in any new horses and Big Sam will get put down and Old Ned and –'

Lucy was stung by this unfairness. 'Don't say that! Course I care! I want to do it as much as you.'

'You only want to do the jumping. You don't really care about R-R-Rosevale and all the h-h-horses!'

'I do!'

But Kitty wouldn't be comforted. Lucy hadn't even the heart to ride Puzzle. What was the point, if they weren't going to do the competition?

She gloomed home down the lane, kicking savagely at the weeds, not letting herself look at Old Ned on the way past.

At home, Lucy heated up the lasagne that had been left beside the microwave. Mum was in her study, and Dad's car wasn't in the drive. The house was very quiet. Lucy hated quiet. She remembered the other night at Cam's, the lovely ringing clatter of five horses trotting over the road.

Five horses.

Well, she could only ask. What was the worst Cam could say? She set the half-eaten lasagne down and went for the yellow pages. Cam's number was easy to find – Old Mill Stables.

When Cam answered, Lucy felt suddenly shy – after all, it was a bit cheeky of her – but then she thought of Big Sam being put down, of the foals having nowhere dry for the winter, and she took a deep breath and began.

Cam seemed to think for a long time. At least she didn't say no straight off.

'You all have to be from the same yard, don't you?'

'Nobody would know.'

'Lucy. *Everybody* would know. I have a professional reputation to think of. '

'But it's a stupid rule. *Normal* competitions don't have rules like that.'

'*Normal* competitions don't have prizes like that.'

'Oh, Cam! We're so desperate. And we'd have a good chance with you.'

'Let me think.'

There was a tantalising silence. Then – 'Does Declan have a spare stable?'

'Yes!' Lucy nearly squeaked. 'The skewbald cob left yesterday.'

'So Ty could come to you on livery until after the competition.' Cam seemed to be thinking out loud. 'That would take care of that rule. Mind you, Declan won't have time to do an extra horse, and I can't come over twice a day when I have my own yard to run ...'

'I'll do him! At least – well, I'm not allowed before school, but I can muck out when I get home, and bring him in and everything. I'm sure Declan wouldn't mind seeing to him in the mornings. Oh, Cam, please!'

Another long silence. Then she said, 'Well, I'll give Declan a ring. How would that be?'

And when Lucy got to the yard next day after school there was a new head looking out over the half door of what had been the skewbald's stable. A bay head with long inquisitive ears and an anxious expression.

'Ty!' Lucy stretched out her hand and stroked his nose. 'You've come to save the day!'

'LUCY?' Erin came up to the wall where Lucy was waiting for Jade and Miranda to come out of the changing rooms after PE. They always took much longer than she did, fussing with their hair.

'Hiya.' She moved over to let Erin sit down.

'D'you want to come to my granda's new house on Saturday?' Erin asked.

'Um ... why?'

'I told you he was getting me a pony. I'm going to keep it at his new house. I thought you might like to come and see the place.'

She hugged her schoolbag. She looked – Lucy searched in her head for the right word – shifty. As if she wasn't quite telling the truth. Well, Lucy didn't quite believe in the pony-buying granda. It sounded more like the kind of thing you'd say because you wanted it to happen. People who lived where Lucy lived didn't *have* pony-buying grandfathers. Lucy liked Erin but she didn't want to waste a precious Saturday visiting some old man in a bungalow with a scruffy paddock out the back.

She suddenly saw her way out of the invitation. 'Saturday. Aw, that's Jade's party,' she said.

'So are you invited?' Erin gave Lucy a very direct look.

'Um ... well, not exactly. She did mention it but –' Lucy chewed her lip. Part of her would have loved, when Jade did get around – soon, she hoped – to inviting her to the party, to say, sorry, she'd made other plans: Jade should have given more notice. But Lucy knew she wouldn't say it.

64

But what if Jade *never* invited her? Wouldn't going to Erin's granda's be better than sitting at home thinking about everybody at the party?

'Can I let you know?' she asked. 'It's only Tuesday.'

Erin stared at her. 'So, let me get this right. You'll come if you don't get a better offer?'

'I didn't mean that.'

'Forget it,' Erin said. 'You might let that snobby cow mess you around, but I won't let you mess *me* around.'

She picked up her schoolbag and walked off just as Jade and Miranda came round the corner from the gym, their long ponytails swinging.

Later that day Jade invited Lucy to her party.

Chapter 10

The Forbidden Field

AIDAN became Ty's stable boy. Lucy had promised to do it, since the whole thing had been her idea, but on the second morning they got up to find Ty solemnly munching shrubs in the front garden. Lucy had forgotten to put the clip in the bolt of the stable door. She apologised a hundred times and promised to be more careful, but Aidan's dad said they couldn't take the risk with someone else's horse. After a couple of days the big goofy-looking bay would stick his head over his half-door and neigh as soon as he heard the back door.

'That's your contribution to the team,' his dad said one evening, when Aidan was pushing a towering, smelly wheelbarrow across the yard.

Looking after Ty was easy compared to watching everybody become more and more obsessed with the team.

'You're sulking cause you're not in it,' Kitty said, the first Saturday in October. They were in the tack room and Aidan had said he couldn't stay and put the jumps up in the school; he was going out on Firefly.

'*I* was the one who said I didn't *want* to be in it,' Aidan retorted, lifting Firefly's saddle down from the rack.

Kitty said nothing.

And it was rubbish, Aidan thought, riding along the trail between the bottom field and the empty field, standing up in his stirrups so he could see over the hedge to where Big Sam was drinking from the stream. He *wasn't* sulking.

Although it was October now and cool in the high-hedged, brambly lane, a thin bright sun warmed the fields, so that Old Sam's mottled rump glowed. Firefly swung along easily and took advantage of being on a loose rein, snatching a late blackberry from the hedge. Aidan laughed and patted him.

'This is much more fun than doing that stupid cross-country, isn't it?' he said. But a sudden memory scratched at him – not, for once, of his own awful failure, but of Firefly cantering easily down the wide slope of Cam's field, with Lucy riding him expertly over the downhill jump. The lift and reach and the confident landing – Firefly had looked as if he enjoyed it all.

Only not with you, *Ponyboy. Because you're too pathetic.*

Hoof-beats clattered behind him, making Firefly tense and alert. Aidan turned in surprise. He normally had the trails to himself.

It was Kitty and Lucy. 'We're just cooling the ponies down,' Kitty said. Lucy gave a half smile. She and Aidan weren't exactly *not speaking*. But not exactly speaking either. 'Cam said they needed a change of scene. And guess what – Cam's bringing up loads of her jumps for us!'

When Lucy spoke it was to Kitty. 'Why's that field empty?' she asked.

Kitty shrugged. 'Dunno. It hasn't been used all year. Something about resting it. Or drainage. Something boring.'

Lucy stood in her stirrups and stretched up for a better view. 'You could put jumps in there. It's got a nice slope. It'd be perfect.'

'Well, we're going to Cam's tomorrow to train on her cross-country,' Kitty said importantly. 'Aidan, did you hear?' She turned round in the saddle. 'We're going to Cam's.'

'Great,' Aidan said in the most enthusiastic voice he could. *See?* that voice was meant to say, *I am not sulking.*

Only he might have overdone it because Kitty said, 'Well, there's no need to be sarcastic. And Dad says you have to come too. So there.'

OK, maybe he was sulking now. Just a bit.

Because this was a stupid waste of his time. There was stuff he could have been doing in the yard – more important stuff than this. September needed more handling, for one thing. She'd come on so well that Dad was hoping they could get her re-homed before the real winter set in, but she was very head-shy, ducking from any attempt to touch her ears.

But he hadn't been given a choice.

'We could do with an extra hand with the horses,' Dad said, 'and you can make yourself useful opening gates and things.'

From what Aidan remembered, there were only a couple of gates: it was just a ploy to make him go back to the scene of his humiliation. He wasn't stupid.

Actually it took half an hour to load Ty, and he and Folly were both bad travellers, upsetting each other and arriving sweaty and twitching. When Ty realised he was back at his old yard he started to neigh at the top of his voice and prance like an eejit, so Aidan had his hands full until Cam rushed up to claim her horse.

'Sorry,' she panted. 'Lesson went on a bit. Thanks, Aidan.'

Standing on the course beside the first jump, he

shrugged himself into his anorak and prepared to be cold and bored for hours.

Cam seemed to have taken over as the *chef d'équipe*. She was more patient than his dad, and it was funny to hear her telling him off. 'Don't let her rush so much, Declan!' Cam called out more than once. His dad was very meek about it, but then he'd had lessons from Cam for years and years when he was young. Aidan liked watching Tyrone jump. Being his stable lad had given him a special interest in the horse, who jumped carefully and suspiciously at first, but then started to relax and enjoy himself. Aidan could see Cam's riding, quiet and consistent, with split-second timing, was giving the young horse confidence. Just as Lucy's riding had given Firefly that night. He pushed that thought away where it couldn't nag him.

The mood in the lorry going home was jubilant. Even Folly and Ty, tired with their efforts and knowing they were going home to warm beds and evening feeds, pulled at their hay-nets and didn't fret.

'When can we go again, Dad?' Kitty asked.

Dad frowned. 'It's hard to get the time. There's not much light these evenings. Cam has lessons at weekends. And Folly and Ty are such bad travellers.'

'But they need to get used to it before the competition,' Kitty argued.

'And we can't practise cross-country without *riding* cross-country,' Lucy added. 'Can we not put jumps in the empty field?'

'No.'

'But Dad, why not?' Kitty whined.

'One, I don't want the ground messed up with galloping hooves. I'm putting the foals out there for the winter, before the barn falls down on top of them. Two, the going's too soft. That field's always boggy and after the wet summer ... Anyway. No.'

Lucy and Kitty looked at each other and both opened their mouths to argue. Then they seemed to think better of it. But Aidan recognised Lucy's determined look. Which, funnily enough, was very like his dad's.

He had a feeling *no* wouldn't be enough for her.

Chapter II

Lucy's Secret

LUCY kicked Puzzle into a trot and checked her watch. How could they only have been out for ten minutes? It felt like hours. Hacking round these lanes was so *boring*. Lots of slow road work, Declan and Cam had ordered. Lots of schooling. *Not* jumping all the time. And goodness knew when they would get back to Cam's. It was Friday evening now and she was busy with lessons all weekend.

'But we need to practise cross-country!' Kitty had protested.

'The Sunnyside team are cross-countrying every day,' Lucy added. This wasn't actually true but she thought it might goad Declan into thinking Rosevale must keep up. But he had only said, 'More fool them,' and carried on mixing feeds.

The team, with Cam, was shaping up really well. Ty had discovered a passion for cross-country, and Cam had begun talking about eventing him. Only Kitty would do the smaller jumps, which meant the other three could go for maximum points and theirs would be the score that counted.

In her most optimistic moments, Lucy thought they had a chance of the five thousand pounds.

But not like this, she gloomed. *Boring old hacking.*

Puzzle's ears pricked, catching Lucy's frustration, but he trotted steadily on. It wasn't so bad when Declan and Cam came and they could go on the actual roads, but they were busy today, so Lucy had to ride alone and stick to the lanes because both her parents and Declan banned her from riding on the roads by herself. She would have welcomed even Aidan's company, but Aidan was fussing round September, who was waiting for the blacksmith to trim her hooves.

She turned right into the lane that wound past the empty field. There it was, bright green, smooth and lovely, much nicer than the poached fields on either side which had been grazed all summer and were now bare and exhausted. It was a biggish field, a little steeper than Cam's. It was a field made for cross-country. If only there was something to jump.

Well, maybe there was. The field was surrounded by a high hedge, with trees here and there. Some fallen branches lay round the edges. Nothing jumpable on its own, but surely with a bit of squidging together she could make at least a couple of jumps?

Lucy kicked her feet out of her stirrups, pulled Puzzle's reins over his head and led him to the gate. Like most of Rosevale's gates it had seen better days and needed a bit of persuasion to open. Puzzle didn't help, nudging it and running backwards and then trying to graze, and she might have given up were it not for the prospect of riding cross-country.

After all, she was doing it *for* Rosevale. Cam and Declan were wrong not to let them practise jumping more. It was OK for them – they were old and had lots of experience. She and Kitty needed all the practice they could get. But even as she picked among the fallen branches, Puzzle grazing quite happily beside her, Lucy knew she couldn't risk telling Kitty. It wasn't fair to drag her into something that would only get her in trouble with Declan if they were caught.

And besides, said a little voice inside her, *you don't think it's so important for Kitty to practise, do you? As long as you do?*

And, the little voice went on, *what you really want is the thrill of galloping and jumping. The team is just an excuse.*

Rubbish! said Lucy's own voice, *it's for Rosevale. And once the foals are turned out in here you'll have lost your chance, so get on with it!*

A hot and breathless twenty minutes later her hands burned with prickles and her shoulders throbbed, but she had made a course. Well, two jumps, but she could jump them both in both directions so that was four jumps really and – if she was brave enough – one of them would be a fairly steep downhill.

The trouble was it was nearly dark. There was so little time for riding these evenings. Could she risk leaving the jumps up until tomorrow? She knew that if Declan saw them they were doomed. But Declan wasn't going to come out here at this time of the evening, and tomorrow was Saturday. There was nothing to stop her getting up really early and riding over them then. She raced through the logistics in her mind – she'd have to lug her tack home, because Declan always locked the tack room at night, but she could pretend she was cleaning it. She would also sneak Puzzle an extra-big feed to make sure he was full of energy for his early-morning ride.

She caught Puzzle, who'd enjoyed his unexpected snack, and rode slowly back to the yard.

'Thought you'd got lost,' Declan said, coming out of Midge's stable, from where she could hear shoeing noises.

'*You* said lots of slow work,' Lucy said innocently. '*You* said it wasn't all about raking and jumping.'

'I didn't say let your pony gorge himself with grass.'

'I didn't –'

75

'His mouth's all green froth. See – you've no talent for crime if you can't hide the evidence.'

He was joking – he grinned at her and gave Puzzle a friendly pat – but Lucy, knowing what she was planning, felt her face flush.

Maybe she wouldn't do it.

But if she didn't, she'd have to get up early anyway to dismantle the jumps.

So she might as well have her fun.

WHEN her phone buzzed at seven, the first thing Lucy heard was the steady drum of rain on the conservatory roof under her window.

Damn! Maybe she wouldn't bother. Her bed was so warm and cosy.

Don't be feeble, she thought. Ten minutes later, having left a note for her parents – AT STABLES. BACK SOON – and grabbed a couple of apples – one each for her and Puzzle – she was letting herself out the back door as quietly as she could, balancing her saddle over her arm. She was glad she hadn't actually got around to cleaning it when she saw the rain dotting it now.

Rosevale was quiet in the dawn light, the barn a mere grey heap, and all the house windows dark. The horses were in at night now, so all she had to do was give Puzzle a quick groom and tack him up. He nickered, expecting his breakfast, but he had to be content with his apple. She threw some haylage in to Ty, Midge and Firefly, the only horses in that part of the yard, to keep them quiet.

'You can have yours afterwards,' she promised Puzzle, slipping the bridle over his head.

Riding out of the yard would be the trickiest bit – there was no disguising the ring of horseshoe on concrete – but she'd decided that if she met anyone she'd say she was giving Puzzle an early-morning hack because she had a party to go to later. After all, he was *her* pony – it wasn't as if she was doing anything wrong. She planned to dismantle the jumps straight afterwards, even though that would be a pity after her hard work last night. Still, she could hide the branches in the hedge. It would be comforting just to know they were there.

Overnight, the jumps had grown in Lucy's imagination to the size and solidity of an Olympic course. It was almost a shock to see, in the drizzling grey dawn, two higgledy-piggledy homemade piles of brush and branch in a boggy field. Still, jumps were jumps.

She didn't want to ride round the field too much – every hoof-print would show. Hopefully Puzzle would be fairly well warmed up from the hack up the lane anyway. She trotted round the edge, but after Puzzle stumbled once or twice she realised it was too dark in the hedge's shadow, and took him out to the centre of the field. With luck the rain would wash away their prints.

After his initial surprise, Puzzle caught Lucy's mood, and when she pushed him into canter he responded eagerly with the toss of his head and the grab for the bit that meant he was in one of the occasional strong moods that Lucy loved. Still, when the canter threatened to become a gallop, Lucy sat down and hauled on the reins in a way she wouldn't have dared do if Cam or Declan were watching, and turned him for the first jump.

It was a pile of brush, about halfway up the slope. Puzzle didn't seem over-impressed, scarcely lifting his hooves enough to clear it the first time.

'Pick up your feet,' Lucy told him, with a smack from her whip. Maybe she had made it a bit puny. Maybe she should have persuaded Kitty to come after all – having someone to put the jumps up made things easier as well as more fun. Now the jump was scattered and looked just like a pathetic heap of branches. She would have to think of it as a spread, Lucy decided, riding Puzzle in a wide circle.

Next time, he jumped better, really stretching himself to clear the whole thing. They left it behind and circled back down the field and up the other side for the solider and bigger of the jumps. Puzzle cleared this one easily, jumping, in fact, so big that Lucy lost a stirrup, and was reaching for it, half-laughing, when Puzzle lowered his head and galloped flat out to the top of the field. Once she had her balance, Lucy just enjoyed it, the wind whipping tears out of her eyes, mud flying into them. Even the rain misting her face was part of it.

This is magic, she thought, *the best feeling in the world – speed and power and your own pony, fit and keen. How can Aidan not want to do this? What is there to be scared of?*

Lucy steadied Puzzle at the crest of the hill and crossed the top of the field at a more controlled pace. In her imagination, she was in the competition. *Lucy McBride from Rosevale on her own Puzzle turns for the last jump, the treacherous downhill. This is the jump that's caused so much trouble here today. If Lucy clears this she's won the day for the Rosevale team, and on her form there doesn't seem to be anything to worry about. The slope is steeper than she realised, but this is a winning combination ...*

Afterwards, though she went over it until her mind ached, Lucy was never sure exactly what had happened. One minute Puzzle was cantering down the hill towards the jump, as enthusiastic as she was.

He went to take off, seemed to hesitate – or maybe he skidded in the wet grass – corrected himself and threw himself over. Lucy sat still, gave him plenty of rein and waited for his usual smooth landing. But his front legs came down heavily and he pecked, his head nearly touching the ground. Lucy just had time to think, in a surprisingly calm way, *I'm coming off, over his head – at least this is a soft landing*, when he righted himself with a snort and trotted on.

They'd got away with it! Lucy let Puzzle trot to the bottom of the field, then slowed him to a walk. They were both sweating.

'Good boy!' Lucy leant forwards and clasped her hands round his steaming neck. She wouldn't tempt fate by jumping any more. She leapt off and let Puzzle graze while she got rid of the evidence by dismantling the jumps. As she rolled the last branch under the hedge she was flushed, not just with physical effort, but also with triumph.

She got back to the hustle and activity of Rosevale's morning routine. Aidan, wearing a huge red anorak though the rain had slackened, was walking across to the near paddock with Ty's lead rein in one hand and Firefly's in the other. It was funny, Lucy thought: Aidan couldn't – or wouldn't – do what she had just been doing, but *she* wouldn't feel happy leading two horses at once. Declan appeared from the barn with a full wheelbarrow. He looked up at the sound of Puzzle's hooves and frowned.

'Been out *already?*'

'You said he needed more quiet hacking.' This wasn't a lie – Declan *had* said so – so Lucy didn't know why she felt suddenly so uncomfortable. 'Plus I'm going to a party this afternoon,' she went on, as if Declan was the slightest bit interested in her social life.

If Declan hadn't been there she would have given Puzzle's legs a good long hosing with cold water – just in *case* he'd given himself a bit of a twist at that bad landing. But she didn't want to draw attention to herself, so she just jumped off, led him into his stable and untacked him. He was damp with a mixture of sweat and rain, so she put his fleece cooler on to dry him off and filled his net with haylage. He attacked it greedily, bashing the net against the wall the way he did when he was extra-hungry.

'I'll be back to put him out when I've had my breakfast,' Lucy said. She could have stayed and helped – there was always plenty to do – but she was starving. That apple felt like a long time ago.

And maybe she didn't want to hang around in case someone questioned her more closely about her ride.

Still, whatever happened, it had been brilliant, galloping and jumping like that all on her own. Worth getting up early for.

Unusually, there was nobody about when she went back around eleven. Apart from Puzzle, the horses were all out in the small paddocks near the yard which Declan used for winter turnout, letting the bigger fields rest. Puzzle had dried off nicely, so Lucy threw his outdoor rug on and led him to the gate. Usually when he was turned out in the morning he had a roll and then a dash round, kicking up his heels after the long night in the stable. But today he just had a long drink from the trough, looked round to see his friends and mooched over to them in a lackadaisical way.

Tired with jumping and galloping, thought Lucy. *With raking,* said that uncomfortable voice – but that was daft. She hadn't been *raking* – she'd been *practising.*

She mucked out quickly, mixed up Puzzle's evening feed and filled his hay-net. Kitty or Aidan would bring him in later.

Jade's party was at the ice rink, which normally Lucy loved, but first of all Jade got in a mood because Lucy was a better skater, and then Josh – whose party it was too, of course – and his stupid friends started showing off and picking on Miranda because she kept falling over, and Miranda cried and wanted to go home before the pizza. The Sunnyside girls were all snobs, who kept saying things like, 'You keep your pony at a *sanctuary*? With *rescue* horses? Are you not worried he'll *catch* something?'

For the first time she thought, *Even if we don't win the money, it'll be worth going to the competition just to show ignorant people like this what rescue horses can do.*

All in all she'd probably have had more fun at Erin's granda's. There was no reception in the ice rink, so it was only when she was waiting on the wall outside for her mum to pick her up that she saw Kitty's text:

PUZ V V LAME!!!! DAD GONNA GET VET. CUM UP AS SOON AS U CAN!!!!!

Chapter 12

A Change of Pony

GEORGE, the vet, gave his verdict. Strained tendons in the near-fore. Most likely incurred galloping or jumping on soft ground.

Dad frowned at Aidan. 'How could that be? Cam's cross-country isn't particularly soft – not soft enough to cause that kind of injury. And it's funny it's just showing up now.'

Aidan shrugged. He was only here to hold the pony.

'It can happen in the field,' George said. 'It's just one of those things.'

Dad shook his head. 'He's turned out on pretty firm ground.'

George clapped Puzzle's shoulder. 'Well, Declan, you know the drill as well as I do. Cold water hosing, often as you can manage it, and box rest. Keep him in for a month and I'll call back and see him then.'

Declan nodded. 'No problem. And while you're here – one of the foals seems to have done something to its eye.'

The men went off across the barn, talking. Aidan thought he might as well start hosing Puzzle's leg now. The cold water would help the swelling and give the pony some relief from the pain. Puzzle didn't stand as quietly as Firefly or September. He kept nudging Aidan, hoping for titbits.

'Spoilt,' Aidan said. 'No, don't eat my zip.' He gave Puzzle a quick bat on the nose and the pony made a grumpy camel face and put his ears back.

'What are you doing to my pony?' It was Lucy, belting up the yard in very fancy clothes, her round face beetroot.

'Thank you very much, Aidan, for hosing my pony's sore leg. Oh, you're welcome, Lucy. No, it's not my job, but I thought I would do it to help you. Here.' He flung the hose at her, not minding at all that it splashed her sparkly leggings.

'Sorry.' Lucy had the grace to look ashamed. 'I was just so worried. What's he done?'

'George is still here.' Aidan indicated the vet, walking towards his Range Rover. 'If you catch him up he can tell you better than me. It's OK – I'll look after Puzzle.'

Lucy handed back the hose and dashed across the yard. Aidan watched the conversation with interest, though he was too far away to hear – George explaining, looking serious, Lucy nodding, then shaking her head hard, staring at the ground, Dad joining in.

'What have you been up to?' he asked Puzzle, and the pony snorted and head-butted him. If he'd been somewhere he shouldn't have been, he wasn't telling.

'BUT it must have happened *somewhere*,' Aidan's mum said.

'Lucy *swears* she's only jumped him with us,' Dad said. 'Kitty, stop crying for goodness' sake and eat your tea. It's not *your* pony that's hurt.'

'But the t-t-team,' Kitty blubbed.

Aidan munched chips, fried egg and beans, and kept out of the conversation. He might have his suspicions, but he wasn't going to tell tales.

'I'm fed up with this blasted team,' Mum said. 'It's caused nothing but bother as far as I can see. People falling out, extra horses taking up time and space, and I hate seeing you so worried. You work hard enough. You don't need any more hassle.' She slid her hand across the table and touched Dad's hand.

Dad gave a long sigh. The zizz which had affected him while the team had been going so well seemed to have deserted him.

'You could be right, Seaneen. It was probably daft. It was just the thought of the money.'

Mum gave a little snort. 'Didn't you say there were

86

dozens of teams entering? You'd have a better chance doing the lottery.'

Exactly what Aidan had always thought, but he had a special reason for not saying anything just now. Because the last thing he wanted was for Kitty to pipe up, '*Aidan* will have to ride instead.' Not that he would – not, he admitted, that he *could* – but it was much safer for the words not even to be spoken aloud.

After tea, Aidan said, 'I'm going to take Alfie for a walk.'

'Don't stay out too long,' Mum said. 'It's nearly dark.'

'I'll just go up the lane a bit.'

Alfie was very much Dad's dog, haunting his heels and regarding the rest of the human race as distinctly second-best, but he shifted his pointed grey muzzle from between his paws and trotted out happily enough at the word *walk,* leaving his basket empty for Bernard to sneak into for warmth.

The lanes and fields were darkening fast, and the air chilled Aidan's face. Alfie, a leggy grey shadow in the dusk, spiralled in delight at the smells the rain had teased out. There was enough light, however, helped out by his torch, for Aidan to see what he had expected to see in the empty field.

Hoof-prints. Scattered twigs in two places, and the sort of churned up ground that can only be made by a horse jumping.

ALTHOUGH it was practically next door, Aidan had never been inside Lucy's house before. It was, as he'd imagined from the pristine white exterior, the exact opposite of his own house: everything very new and shiny and matching. And *quiet*. Lucy herself was so noisy and enthusiastic that it was hard to imagine her coming from here.

Her parents were apparently both in – their gleaming cars were parked on the weedless tarmac drive – but the whole time he was there he didn't see or hear them. His own mum would have been rushing to see who had come in, and making cups of tea and opening biscuit tins. Lucy's kitchen, all steel and chrome and glass, didn't look as if it contained biscuit tins, much to the disappointment of Alfie, who sank down at Aidan's heels with a sigh.

'What is it?' Lucy asked. 'Is Puzzle worse?' Like Kitty's, her face was swollen with crying.

'He's fine, as far as I know.' Aidan dug his hands deeper into the pocket of his jeans. Having decided to come and force a confession from Lucy, he wasn't sure how to start – or exactly *why.* He coughed, pulled one of Alfie's ears gently, took out his phone and fiddled with it until he had what he wanted. 'Look,' he said. 'I want to know why you're lying about jumping Puzzle in the empty field.'

Lucy's face flamed. 'I didn't ... I never ... I was only ...'

Aidan showed her his phone. The pictures weren't terribly clear – it had been almost dark and he'd had to use the flash – but it was obvious what they were – the take-off and landing of improvised cross-country jumps.

'Scroll through if you like. I took a few.'

When Lucy looked up, her face was ashamed. 'Are you going to tell your dad?' she whispered.

'I'm not a *tell-tale*,' Aidan said in disgust.

'So why –'

'I just don't know why *you* didn't tell him! Everybody's been going round and round in circles thinking *how* it could have happened, and now Dad's worrying about the drainage in the paddocks, and Mum's worried about Dad, and Kitty's crying about the team and – I don't know, Lucy – I just didn't think *you* were such a coward.'

'It was only *once*. For, like, twenty minutes or something. I never – if I'd known ...' She bit her lip but at least she didn't burst into tears. He'd had enough of that with Kitty.

Aidan waited. Lucy picked at a non-existent bit of dirt on her jumper.

'I'm scared to tell your dad,' she admitted at last. 'He was *so* angry about Ty's door. You didn't hear him. I feel sick every time I think about it. He might not even let me stay at Rosevale.' Now she was crying properly. 'S-sorry,' she spluttered. 'I feel so bad – about hurting Puzzle and about letting everybody down.'

And now Aidan's mind admitted the other reason why he had come. 'You don't have to let them down,' he said. 'You can ride Firefly.'

Lucy stared, her blue eyes round. 'Honestly?' she said at last. 'You'd trust me with him, after – after this morning?'

'Well, you're hardly going to do that again, are you?'

She shook her head, sniffing. 'Never. I'll do exactly what Declan and Cam say, I promise.'

'I know. And you ride him really well – better than me.' A cold ball of sadness opened up inside him when he said this.

'Will he be fit enough, though?' Lucy asked with a sudden frown. 'It's only three weeks away.'

'Well, I ride him nearly every day. Mostly hacking, but he's pretty fit. Anyway, see what Dad and Cam say.'

Dad and Cam, predictably, said a lot. So did Kitty and Mum. All of it exceptionally complimentary about Aidan.

How generous he was.

How thoughtful.

How much a team player. Even for a team he wasn't in.

'I'd never have asked you to do that,' his dad said. 'Not your own pony. But I'm really proud of you.'

It was all very gratifying to hear. But it didn't make up for the unexpected pain of seeing Lucy ride Firefly, rather cautiously at first, aware, probably, of having been given this chance only for Rosevale's benefit, but soon with all her usual spark and courage, qualities which seemed to transmit themselves to his pony.

And it definitely didn't silence the nasty little voice inside him which insisted on whispering, *You're not doing it for Lucy. You're not even doing it for Rosevale. You're doing it for yourself.*

Because as long as Lucy was jumping Firefly – brilliantly and bravely – nobody expected Aidan to do it.

AIDAN stood at the top of Cam's field with the stopwatch.

'It's not about *raking*,' Cam said, carefully not looking at Lucy. 'But we need to get a good time, so you *will* need to gallop. When it's *safe*, Lucy.' As always she slipped easily into instructor mode. 'OK, one at a time, down over the logs, and when you get to the bottom, turn and gallop up the hill. Aidan will time you.'

As the competition approached, they had been spending more time at Cam's. Aidan would have preferred not to go, but he couldn't have people saying he was jealous of Lucy. And it was funny how much more involved he felt now that Firefly was in the team. It stung to watch Lucy doing so well on him, but in another way he was proud of his pony. Even now, he was hoping Firefly would be one of the fastest. And it would have been daft to have made the big gesture of lending him, only for Firefly not to have been any good. And in three weeks – two weeks – a week – the competition would be over, and he would have his pony back.

By now the downhill jumps held no fear for any of the team. *Rather them than me,* Aidan thought, as he watched his dad take the jump easily, make a wide arc round the bottom of the field, then give Folly her head to the top. When she was younger – Aidan's dad had rescued her from horrendous abuse – Folly had often galloped flat out, but usually without being asked to. Aidan grinned at her now, keen but controlled, his dad's wiry body crouched over her withers like a jockey, his face mud-spattered under his hat.

Aidan clicked the button. 'Thirty-one seconds,' he announced.

His dad grinned and clapped Folly's white neck. 'Good girl! We can show these youngsters all right.'

Folly's huge nostrils flared red with effort. Dad gave her a long rein while her breath returned to normal. He watched with interest as Kitty took her turn. Thirty-nine seconds, with Midge's little legs going like pistons.

'Good girl,' Dad said, and Kitty grinned at him. Aidan caught the grin and felt suddenly left out.

Wise up. You had your chance. You didn't want to do it.

You mean you can't *do it, Ponyboy!*

Chapter 13

Another Brilliant Idea

THE days galloped towards the competition and Lucy had never been so busy. She took to cycling to the yard and back, just to save a few minutes.

Puzzle, fretful and fed up, took a lot of time and care. Every time Lucy saw his head looking sadly over the stable door at his friends out in the paddocks, she had a fresh rush of guilt. Puzzle was bored and becoming naughty – nipping her and biffing her with his nose if she didn't have titbits, fiddling incessantly with the clip on the bolt on his door, and restlessly paddling his bed into a messy pulp which made mucking out take three times as long as usual.

If only she'd obeyed Declan, Puzzle would be sound and happy now, and Aidan would have his own pony to ride.

But she loved riding Firefly. After the first few days, they had become used to each other. He needed more encouragement than Puzzle, but he soon began to realise that Lucy, unlike Aidan, was never going to ask him to jump and then change her mind.

'He's the kind of pony who needs you to instil confidence in him,' Cam said one evening after she had given them a private lesson in the school. 'But once he trusts you, he'll do anything for you. And he's talented. You and Puzzle were good, but I think you and Firefly *could* be even better.'

'Only because he's bigger.' Lucy wasn't having anyone finding fault with poor hurt Puzzle.

'He's starting to show the kind of form he used to have in his jumping days. He's wasted on Aidan.'

'That's not fair.' Lucy forgot how often she had thought the same thing herself. 'Aidan loves him.'

'Yes, but the pony could be doing so much more. Anyway, he's getting his chance now. Just make the most of it.' And, with a quick pat on Firefly's shoulder, she headed off to her jeep.

Lucy dismounted and ran the stirrups up. It was darkish in the yard after the floodlit school and she didn't realise Aidan was standing beside her until Firefly's nostrils gave a low welcoming flutter. Lucy hoped he hadn't heard what Cam had said.

'I'll put Firefly in,' he said, taking the reins.

Lucy hesitated. It was up to Aidan, of course – she wasn't going to tell him he couldn't put his own pony to bed – but she didn't want him thinking she expected to have the fun of riding Firefly without any of the work.

'I don't mind,' she said.

'I want to.'

'OK. He's going really well.'

'I know.'

There wasn't much she could answer to this. It was awkward, feeling so grateful. She couldn't keep on and on saying *thank you*. And it wasn't *just* gratitude. There was the shaming fact that Aidan was the only person who knew about the forbidden field, and he hadn't told Declan. Lucy *was* going to confess, of course, just – well, just not yet.

'I wish there was something I could do to kind of *show* him I'm grateful – well, all of them, really,' she said to her mum when she got home and was meant to be doing her English homework. 'Declan hoses Puzzle's leg in the mornings when I'm at school.'

'We're paying extra for that,' said her mum, who had no idea how busy Declan was.

Her mum didn't know about her letting Ty out, or that Puzzle's injury was Lucy's fault. She had accepted Lucy's story that it was just bad luck. Lucy's dad had grumbled about the vet's bill, but otherwise her parents, as usual, hadn't shown much interest.

'Even so. If there was something ...'

'Just help them to win.' Her mum made it all sound easy.

But next day, when Lucy arrived home from school, there was a brand-new cross-country top sitting on her bed. Red and blue quarters, with a hat silk to match. She turned the top over. ROSEVALE was embroidered across the back. And piled up in their plastic wrapping, three identical tops – a little one for Kitty and adult-size ones for Declan and Cam. Lucy flew downstairs.

'Now we'll look like a proper team. You're brilliant, Mum.' She gave her mum a quick hug and raced off to the yard to see to Puzzle, ride Firefly and show everyone their posh new kit.

And of course they loved it.

But it hadn't even been Lucy's idea. And though it was definitely something for Rosevale, it still wasn't for Aidan. She would have to come up with something better.

AS far as Lucy could see, Olly and Josh didn't vary their routine much: a foot stuck out from under a desk as Aidan walked past, a whispered *Ponyboy* when Miss Connor called his name in registration, *GAY* scribbled in black marker on his locker door, an over-enthusiastic rugby tackle. Actually Lucy only guessed at the rugby tackling because of the way Aidan always looked a bit battered on a Wednesday after PE.

More battered today than usual.

'Ouch,' Lucy said, as Aidan joined her on the bus and she saw the purplish bruise spreading across his cheekbone. 'Who did that?'

'Nobody,' Aidan said, glancing behind him.

'You know you should –'

'I said it was nobody.'

Lucy gave up and satisfied herself with giving Olly and Josh her nastiest look, which was totally wasted on them.

If only they could see how capable Aidan was around the yard, she thought, frowning out the window at the drizzling grey of the late afternoon and hoping the weather would improve by Saturday. The trouble was, they'd decided it was girly to be into horses. (Well, how could they think anything else, when they were used to Jade and Sunnyside?) They had no idea of the real hard work that went on. If they could see some of the things Lucy saw Aidan doing: helping Declan calm a thrashing, plunging, terrified horse, hammering in fence posts, leading several horses together.

Was it time to tell Kitty what was going on? She would tell her parents and they would do something about it.

As soon as Lucy arrived at the yard that afternoon, before she'd even said hello to Puzzle, Kitty beckoned her into the little building where the small ponies were stabled.

'Come and see this,' she whispered.

This was September stretched out in her stable with her head on Aidan's knee. Her tiny hooves peeped from under her. She still had a pinkish tinge but was starting to get fluffy. Aidan was stroking her ears and talking to her in a low, soothing voice.

'Good girl. See, nobody's going to hurt your silly old ears. Clever pony. ' He was so absorbed that he clearly hadn't noticed the girls watching.

Lucy whipped out her phone and took the photo without thinking.

'Ah, will you send me that?' Kitty whispered. 'My phone's in the house.'

'Course I will.'

Aidan and September looked up at the sound of voices, and the pony scrambled to her feet.

And Lucy had a brilliant idea.

By the end of the evening Lucy's phone had been busy, and she had quite a gallery of Rosevale life. In bed she scrolled through the photos, deleting the duds, sending Kitty the one of September. She thought she'd been pretty clever. There were photos of Aidan grooming Big Sam – all eighteen hands of him – lunging Ty in the school, and a great one of him carrying a huge sack of feed over one shoulder. She bet Olly and Josh, rugby stars though they might be, couldn't do any of those things.

She couldn't just rush up to them, show them the photos and say, 'Look, isn't Aidan Kelly brave and capable and worthy of your respect and wouldn't you like to leave him alone?' Subtlety wasn't Lucy's strong suit, but she wasn't that dense. No. Somehow she would have to work through Jade. Jade would have to say something to Josh. Not that she could *tell* Jade the plan. She would have to just show her the photos and play it by ear.

At break-time Lucy and her friends crowded round their special place.

'We're all having plaits on Saturday,' Jade said, opening her lunchbox and taking out her usual snack of perfectly cut carrot sticks.

'You or the ponies?' asked Lucy.

'Both.'

With purple elastics, no doubt, Lucy thought, but she didn't want to waste the precious few minutes of break talking about hair and mane styling.

'I took some new photos,' she said, taking out her phone. As predicted, they all gathered round.

'What do *you* want, Erin?' Jade asked.

'To get to my locker. *If* it's OK by your majesty.' Erin

stalked past, her red bob swinging. Lucy gave her a small apologetic smile.

'Ah, look at the wee foals,' Miranda said. 'Why are they all in together? And have they no mummies? That's really cruel.'

Lucy explained about the foals.

'There's a good one – if you scroll on a bit – of Aidan grooming Big Sam. He's eighteen-two!' She didn't add that Big Sam was as gentle as a Labrador.

'There's a *lot* of photos of Aidan,' Jade remarked.

Lucy's face burned. 'Well ... he does live there,' she said.

'Ooh, Lucy's gone all red! Lucy fancies Aidan!'

'Shut up, Jade.' Her plan wasn't going too well.

'Oh my goodness!' Miranda gave a sudden squawk. 'That is *so* cute.'

Lucy leant over her shoulder. It was the photo of September. It had come out really well, though the electric light in the stable had made the pony look really quite pink. It was the cutest thing Lucy had ever seen. It was the cutest thing, the girls agreed, that *any* of them had ever seen. They all wanted copies. Even Erin came over to look and exclaim.

'My granda's getting me a pony,' she said.

Jade rolled her eyes.

'Rosevale looks lovely,' Erin went on. 'Do they do lessons? I'm going to start lessons.'

'No,' Lucy said. 'It's not a riding school.' She was about to say that Erin should contact Cam if she wanted lessons – though she couldn't help thinking Cam might be a bit expensive – when Miranda said quickly, 'And they don't take beginners at Sunnyside. Or people without their own ponies. Before you ask.'

'I wasn't going to ask,' Erin said. 'I'm kind of fussy where I go.'

Lucy couldn't help grinning, but she bit it off. She wanted to tell Erin to come to Greenlands on Saturday, but something about Jade and Miranda stopped her. Anyway, she had a more important mission just now.

She sent the photo to all their phones quite happily.

It was only afterwards that she had a faint stirring of unease.

A tiny pink pony in the straw, resting her head on his knee. That hadn't been quite the image she had been trying to cultivate for Aidan.

Chapter 14

My Little Ponyboy

OLLY blocked the doorway to the boys' lockers.

'Excuse me,' Aidan said. As always when he didn't want it to, his voice came out thin and high. He wanted to shove Olly out of the way but he knew from experience that Olly would shove back harder.

'My Little Ponyboy. Bless!' Olly said. 'I can't *wait* to see you at the competition tomorrow. Are you sure that pony's not too big for you, though?' He clapped Aidan's cheek in a pretend matey way and swaggered out. 'Oh,' he said, half-turning, as if he'd suddenly remembered something important, 'Josh is just coming. He had a wee bit of decorating to do in there. You'll love it.'

More graffiti about him, he supposed. Maybe he wouldn't bother going to the toilet after all. Or he would ask out of French – Madame Sudret was dead soft – and see what the latest was then.

It wasn't graffiti. And photos could be pulled down, even if you were meant to be in French. Aidan didn't know how Olly and Josh had got hold of the picture of him and September, but he could guess. And by the time he had torn down nine copies of it – four in the boys' toilets, one outside the maths room, one on the library door, and three in the junior boys' lockers – he was ready to kill Lucy. Especially when he didn't get back to French until just before the bell, and Madame Sudret asked in a loud and meaningful whisper if he was sure he was quite well, and everybody laughed.

He shoved his French books into his bag. The tenth photo peeked out from between his geography book and *The Outsiders.*

Between the French room and the top of the stairs down to science there were three more. He wasn't going to tear them down in front of people, so instead he walked straight past the science room, out of the building, down the main driveway and out of the gates. Nobody stopped him.

It wasn't noon yet, and there wouldn't be a school bus for hours, so Aidan walked into the centre of town and caught the normal bus instead.

The yard was empty. His mum was at work but the Land Rover was away too, and the trailer, which must mean Dad had gone to pick up some new animal, though he hadn't mentioned it. Puzzle's head looked out from over his half-door, glad of the distraction. In all the paddocks, horses nosed at tough autumn grass.

He looked into the stables: all mucked out, all the hay-nets filled and tied up for the evening. There was nothing to do and he needed, suddenly, to be doing something. Something that would distract him from those stupid photos, from the trouble he was going to be in for walking out of school. He wandered down to the paddock to see Firefly, hardly noticing the mud clinging to his school shoes. Clipped and in his winter rug, standing beside the gate with a faraway expression in his eyes, his pony looked unfamiliar and smart, his clipped ears nearly transparent. He didn't look like Aidan's pony any more.

'Want to come for a ride?' Aidan asked.

He hadn't brought a head-collar, but Firefly walked placidly beside him with Aidan leading him by the forelock. It comforted Aidan just a little to know he wouldn't have done that for Lucy.

Firefly bustled into his stable and started to pull at the hay-net. From his own stable, lonely Puzzle let out a high-pitched neigh.

'We're going out,' Aidan said, 'so don't fill your belly with hay.' He untied the net and threw it outside, much to the pony's door-kicking disgust. He unrugged Firefly, gave him a quick groom and tacked up. He grabbed his hat and they were off.

He didn't know where they were going. But he needed to be moving and he needed company, and *not* human company.

Aidan had been worried that his pony would feel different after three weeks of Lucy's bolder riding, but, after he adjusted the stirrups, which had been set to suit Lucy's shorter legs, Firefly felt only familiar, walking out with a long stride, snuffing the cold autumn air, glad to be out. The brambles lining the lane were all withered now; the few blackberries clinging on looked sour and nibbled.

Relaxing into the easy swing of Firefly's walk, Aidan tried to forget about school. But everything he tried to distract himself with – Firefly, September, the competition tomorrow – led up the same path, the path that ended with Josh's big red face and his sneery names. *My Little Ponyboy.* And they would be there tomorrow, supporting that annoying Jade.

He knew he couldn't get out of going. OK if they were going to see him jumping huge fences and helping to win the money, but what would they see? A harassed groom, doing all the donkey work. He remembered the day he'd been sick and stayed off school. Could he fake something tomorrow?

As soon as he had the idea, his disgust for himself doubled. Trebled. He leaned forward and straightened Firefly's neat red mane. Honestly, no wonder people thought he was feeble. He hadn't even stayed at school to stick up for himself. He imagined them noticing he had gone. *Ah, wee Ponyboy's run home to his mummy! Wee Ponyboy's cwying.*

He *wasn't* crying. He bashed one hand crossly at his eyes. Firefly, always hyper-sensitive to his rider's moods, started to jog and pull. For once, Aidan was tempted to let him go, to tear up the long lane as fast as they could, to let speed and wind and power hammer out his twisted fears and self-loathing.

But, even after the wet summer, the lane was hard and stony, and Firefly had an important competition next day. And *he* wasn't as stupid as Lucy. Blasted Lucy. He knew where that photo must have come from. If it weren't for Rosevale, he'd tell her she couldn't ride his pony after all.

Aidan turned the pony for home.

The yard was still empty. In the school the jumps were still up from a recent jumping practice, Cam's good painted poles looking solid and forbidding. The gate was open.

'Come on, boy.' Aidan guided Firefly into the school and pushed the pony into trot and then canter. Firefly responded with a tiny buck, but then settled into a lovely fast powerful canter which seemed to eat up the long sides of the school in a few strides. The jumps in the centre flew past in a blur of colour. At first Aidan sat down, pushing the pony on, but after a few circuits he stood in his stirrups and crouched over Firefly's withers as if he were racing or riding cross-country.

'Faster,' he whispered. Firefly plunged into a gallop, his red ears pinned back, stretching and reaching like a racehorse.

It was brilliant. It was the fastest Aidan had ever been, apart from once when a rescue pony had bolted with him. It was powerful and thrilling and –

And a stupid way to ride a pony who was taking part in a competition next day. Aidan knew that, and reluctantly asked Firefly to slow down. The pony was excited, and it took another circuit of the school before the gallop became a canter.

'Aidan?'

He hadn't seen his dad drive into the yard. Dad leant out of the Land Rover window. At a very proper walk, letting Firefly stretch his neck, Aidan rode to the gate.

'There you are,' his dad said, as if he had been half-expecting to see Aidan.

'I was just giving him a bit of exercise,' he said innocently. 'He's still my pony.'

'The school phoned.'

'Oh.' The gallop had worked, because Aidan had briefly forgotten. Now it all flooded back. He opened his mouth to say something – anything – and found that he couldn't.

'I ... something ...' he managed to splutter and gave up. He scratched his cheekbone.

Dad looked hard at him, but all he said was, 'I could do with a hand with this new horse. Untack Firefly and turn him out in the school for ten minutes. He'll cool himself down.'

The new horse came off the ramp like a dervish, a whirl of black flying mane and tail, shrieking.

'Watch yourself, son,' Dad said. 'He's a bit het up.'

At the end of his lead rope the horse reared.

Many of the horses who came to Rosevale were cowed, all spirit beaten or starved out of them. But occasionally there was one like this, whose fear of humans showed in lashing hooves and lunging teeth. Aidan's dad spoke to the horse quietly, gradually shortening the rope until he was standing at the horse's wet shoulder. 'Easy,' he crooned. 'Good lad. Good horse. There's the brave horse.'

It was a black cob of about fifteen hands, thin but not skeletal, with a long tangled mane full of burrs. Recent whip marks and what looked like burns stuck out, red and purple, along his heaving flanks. He stood trembling and snorting, ready to leap and run at the first chance, not knowing there was nowhere to go, not understanding yet that he'd arrived somewhere he'd be cared for.

'I'll lead him if you do the doors and things,' Aidan's dad said to him in the same low tone. 'Isolation stable's ready for him.'

The cob danced across the yard, head high, eyes goggling. It clearly took all Declan's strength to hold him, but he never panicked or faltered, and kept up that running reassurance the whole time. 'Good man, here we go, you can rest here.'

Aidan held open the door of the big isolation stable, but the cob pulled and jerked at the end of the lead rope, not trusting the narrow space. It took both of them, and a lot of false starts, to encourage him in.

'How did you get him onto the horsebox?' Aidan asked his dad, as the cob whirled away from the door a third time.

'Policeman helped. Cruelty case,' Dad said shortly. 'As you can see.'

Finally the cob gave in, plunged into the stable and stood shaking in the far corner. There was a deep bed and a fat hay-net, but he was too upset to acknowledge these yet. Aidan liked it better when the new horses were just hungry, when they would stand knee-deep in the clean bed and pull at the hay-net in stunned delight.

'We'll leave him now,' Dad said. 'He'll settle better on his own. And you and Kitty are *not* to go near him unless I'm with you.'

They walked back to the main yard. In the school, an impatient Firefly was digging up the sand by the gate. He had been rolling and would need a good grooming.

'I'll just get him,' Aidan said.

'He's OK for the moment,' Dad said. 'Now – what happened at school?'

Aidan swallowed. 'How do you know...?'

'Well, something happened or you wouldn't be here, would you?'

Aidan didn't reply. His dad leaned against the sand-school fence, appearing to watch Firefly. He looked, for once, like a man with time on his hands.

'You don't seem so happy at school,' he remarked casually.

Aidan shrugged.

'You haven't mentioned friends or...'

Aidan shrugged.

'Your mum thought you might be having trouble settling.'

Aidan shrugged.

Dad picked at a green smear on the fence post. 'Bit tough being a boy who likes horses?'

Aidan jumped. How did his dad –

Dad scratched his nose. Aidan knew he would have faced a dozen traumatised horses more easily than have this kind of conversation with his son.

'Look, Aidan,' he said at last, 'I don't want you to think ... I mean, just because this – the yard and the horses – is so important to me ... *you* don't have to do it, you know. Your mum thinks I've been forcing you into it.'

Aidan didn't even have to think about the answer. 'You haven't. What we do here – helping horses – I feel the same way you do.' And for all his dad's words, Aidan knew he couldn't manage Rosevale without the help Kitty and especially Aidan gave him.

Aidan turned away from his dad and went into the school. Firefly, bored, came up to him and plunged his head into the waiting head-collar, expecting a feed. Aidan led him to his stable, rubbed him down and checked the time. It was only three o'clock. Might as well turn him out for another few hours. He put on Firefly's outdoor rug and led him to the paddock.

Where his dad was waiting for him.

Aidan sighed. 'Look, Dad, it's fine.'

'And that's why you're at home with your eyes all red, because everything's *fine*?'

'I –'

'It's nothing to be ashamed of, Aidan. When I first got into horses I got a hard time, you know. Lads on the estate calling me Horseboy, saying horses were "gay". And remember, I lived in Belfast. I had to walk through a housing estate wearing jodhpurs.'

'But I'm not *like* you!' Aidan burst out. 'You jumped at Balmoral.'

'What's that got to do with anything?' His dad looked genuinely surprised.

'Because if I was *good* at it, it would be OK. I think. But being called *P-Ponyboy* when you can't even ride properly – it's just so ... so ...' He frowned, wishing he hadn't been so honest, vaguely aware that if it were his mum rather than his dad it would be quite easy just to give up and blub and let her comfort him.

Ah, Ponyboy's cwying to his mummy.

But he didn't want that. He opened the gate and led Firefly through.

Dad sighed. 'You *can* ride properly. What were you doing when I came into the yard? Firefly was going brilliantly.'

'*Lucy's* got him going brilliantly, you mean.'

'It's only confidence, Aidan. I keep telling you.'

'You mean I'm a wuss.' Aidan unbuckled Firefly's head-collar, and the pony plunged away, neighing at his friends.

'I said *confidence* – not *courage*.'

'Same thing. And *you* were the one said you were ashamed of me, that time when I quit the team ...' His voice trailed off. Just to remember his dad's words that terrible morning made his face burn. 'You said you wished I wasn't so ... I was in my room but I heard you – you and Mum.'

His dad frowned. Then smiled. 'Aidan. Look at me.'

He took hold of Aidan's shoulders and made him face him. 'I know what I said. I said I wished you weren't so worried about disappointing me.'

Aidan searched his dad's face. His eyes were dark and honest. Aidan bit his lip. Shrugged. Shook his head. Fiddled with the head-collar rope in his hand.

Aidan's dad massaged his shoulders. 'I've never been ashamed of you. You're my right-hand man on this yard. I keep trying to tell you. And confidence *isn't* the same as courage. You've got plenty of courage. Did you flinch when that cob reared up at you? No. Lucy would have been at the other end of the yard. As for these boys, whoever they are, they wouldn't come within miles of anything like that, would they?

'No,' said Aidan. 'I suppose not.'

Chapter 15

The Row

'DON'T ride Firefly tonight, Lucy,' Declan said, stopping Folly beside Lucy and Puzzle. Lucy looked up in surprise, careful to keep the hose trained on Puzzle's bad leg. Folly stepped back from the jet of cold water, her big black eyes horrified.

'I thought we were giving them all a quiet school just to limber up for the morning?'

'Aidan's already ridden him.'

'What! But it's the competition tomorrow!' Goodness knew what Aidan had done; probably let Firefly mooch along, not paying attention, getting him into bad habits. Why couldn't he have waited one more day?

'Lucy, he *is* Aidan's pony.' Declan's voice was cool. 'We're just having a quick twenty minutes in the school. All you have to do is clean your tack for tomorrow.' He nodded at her and rode on, just as if she wasn't part of their blasted team!

Lucy pouted. So it was *her* tack when it needed cleaning, but it was *Aidan's* pony when he wanted him to be. And this time tomorrow the competition would be over, and Aidan would take Firefly back, and Puzzle would still be lame, and she, Lucy, would have *nothing* to ride. And it was half-term on Wednesday and life would just be dull, dull, dull.

Don't be silly, she told herself. *You're just nervous about tomorrow.* Only that was stupid, because she didn't get nervous. But *something* was twisting her inside and making her feel cross.

And where had Aidan *got* to today? He wasn't sick, and she didn't think he'd had an appointment or anything. She had seen the photo – they all had – but surely nobody would walk out of school just because of a thing like that?

She led Puzzle back to his stable, trying not to let herself see that he was still obviously lame, and then gloomed into the tack-room. Firefly's tack was filthy, spattered with sand as if he'd been raking round the school. With Aidan? And now she was expected to clean it? Unfair. Unfair. Unfair.

She settled herself on the chair in the tack room with the dirty saddle and bridle and her tack-cleaning stuff. She hated cleaning tack. And Firefly's tack was horrible – much older than her own, which meant it needed a lot more work to make it look good enough for a

116

competition. The tedium of tack-cleaning was made worse by the fact that the sound of the others riding in the school drifted in through the open window.

Finally she was done. She hung Firefly's bridle on its hook. Lucy and Kitty had wanted the team all to have brow-bands to match their red and blue tops, but Declan and Cam had said no way. They might, Cam said, be jumping with children, but they weren't going to look like children, and Declan had laughed and Kitty and Lucy had sulked.

Aidan came in, carrying two lots of tack – his dad's and Kitty's.

'Oh,' he said. 'You're in here.'

'I was cleaning Firefly's tack.'

Aidan set the two saddles carefully on their racks and hung up the bridles. He turned as if to leave, then hesitated at the doorway.

'Why did you show people that photo?' he demanded.

'I didn't ... oh.' She bit her lip. 'I sent it to Jade – she must have shown Josh.' She couldn't even start to explain what her original plan about the photos had been. It sounded so lame and, like most of her brilliant ideas, it had backfired. 'I didn't know – I thought it would help.'

'Some help! Butting in, telling the whole class I lived in a – a charity –'

'But that's true!'

'Making me look like I couldn't stick up for myself –'

'Well, you couldn't!' His unaccustomed nastiness surprised Lucy into savagery. 'Look at you – moping around, no friends, too scared to be in the team – you're just *asking* to be bullied.'

Aidan's dark eyes blazed.

Lucy didn't know why he was being so nasty. It could only be jealousy, watching her get ready for the competition *he* hadn't been good enough to do. But two people could be nasty.

'Look, it's not *my* fault you can't ride your own pony.'

'No,' Aidan fired back, 'but it's your fault you can't ride yours, isn't it?'

'What the hell...?' Declan stood in the doorway, two head-collars hanging off his shoulder. 'You two can be heard all over the yard. Do I need to remind you we have a very nervous new horse?'

'Lucy's got something to tell you,' Aidan said, pushing past her. 'Something she was too *scared* to tell you before.'

Lucy's insides turned to ice. 'I ... I ...' she stuttered.

Declan looked bored. 'Lucy, if you're finally going to admit you raked Puzzle in the far field and that's what wrecked his tendons, don't waste your breath.'

Lucy swallowed. 'Did Aidan tell you?' She felt less guilty, now, about saying those nasty things.

'Did Aidan know?' Declan sounded surprised. 'No, I saw for myself when I put the foals out. It's not easy to cover a horse's tracks in a muddy field, especially when you're raking the hell out of it.'

Lucy looked hard at the floor, blinking back tears. Declan had always had the ability to make her feel small, but right now she felt about the size of a mouse. If only she *were* a mouse, she could scuttle through the skirting board and disappear.

'I'd have thought more of you if you'd had the guts to tell me,' he said. He hung up the head-collars and turned to go. 'I want to lock up here now,' he said. 'Make sure you're in good time in the morning – we want to leave at ten.'

LUCY buried her face deeper in Puzzle's lovely springy mane. He blew at her in a friendly way and went straight back to attacking his hay-net. Around them the yard was quiet with only the little snufflings and shiftings and munchings of the horses.

'I'm sorry,' Lucy whispered. 'I know it's my fault. But you'll get better. I promise you'll get better and we'll be riding and jumping and having fun again, and maybe we'll go to the beach some day.'

But a permanently lame pony hobbled through her imagination.

She imagined she heard George, the vet's, voice: 'I'm sorry; the damage is permanent.' And her dad: 'We can't keep a useless pony. He'll have to be put down.'

These were the thoughts she didn't usually allow herself, the thoughts she could keep away by concentrating on the competition. Everything was focused on that one event. Beyond that she couldn't let herself think.

But now, after the horrible row, and realising that Aidan despised her much more than she despised him, and Declan saying she had no guts, the magic distraction wasn't working.

Her phone pinged. *Your tea is ruined! Home NOW!!!*

She supposed she should go. Staying here, torturing herself, was only making her feel worse. And Puzzle was happy with his hay-net. It wasn't as if he was in agony. And maybe, after all, George would say, 'He's doing really well; he'll be good as new in no time.'

She let herself out quickly, grabbed her bike from where she'd left it and jumped on. It had no lights. She'd have to sneak in without her mum realising she'd been cycling or there'd be another row.

In the house behind the yard, a warm light glowed in the window of the room where the Kellys did most of their living. It was a big untidy room with a huge old range and squashy chairs that usually had cats curled up in their shabby depths. Lucy's mum, on the one occasion she had been in it, had said it was a hovel. Lucy loved it, but she had a horrible feeling she wouldn't be welcome there any more. She imagined them all talking about her, laughing at her: *Silly Lucy, thinking we didn't know. What a* coward!

She wished she could go in, say she was sorry, admit she had indeed been too cowardly to own up. But her stomach twisted sickly at the very idea.

She would just go home and have her tea and a good sleep, and next day she would ride for Rosevale and be so brilliant, so instrumental in winning that five-thousand-pound prize for the yard, that everything would be forgiven.

Her wheels whirred through the darkness. Scuds of wind pushed clouds across the moon so that sometimes moonlight brightened the pitted lane. Other times she had to rely on luck as she pedalled through darkness. But the lights of her own house guided her, and she arrived home safely. Tea and TV, a bath steaming with bubbles and a hot chocolate in bed went a long way towards making her feel better. And after all, she thought, banging her pillow into a more comfortable position, the competition is the perfect chance to make amends to everyone, *and* to show the Sunnyside girls that Rosevale is a much better yard. And Puzzle will probably be fine.

Puzzle ... something about Puzzle. On the edge of sleep she remembered him munching his hay. And herself racing off at her mum's text. And closing the door behind her. She remembered kicking the kick-bolt home – she *thought* – but what about the bolt itself? Suddenly wide awake, she forced her memory through her leaving of the stables. But no matter how many times she went over it, her memory refused to give her the reassuring click of the clip being put in to secure the bolt.

HER bike having no lights was actually an advantage. Even if someone happened to be looking out the windows at Rosevale, they wouldn't see her. With coat and wellies pulled on over pyjamas and socks, she pedalled furiously up the drive, trying to avoid the potholes which the moon obligingly picked out for her, her mind flitting between certainty that she *must* have closed the door properly and horror that she hadn't, that Puzzle, bored after finishing his hay, had managed to let himself out – was even now rampaging round the yard or grazing along the lane or – she couldn't bear to think of this but her brain tortured her with it – already on the road, with the cars.

Here was the yard, dark and silent. No lights shone from the downstairs windows of the house, only upstairs. They must all have gone to bed early because of the big day ahead. Lucy left her bike against the wall and slipped round to the main stable block. There were a few surprised low nickerings at her approach but the steady happy chomp told her that the horses were still eating and not likely to kick up a fuss. She didn't dare turn the lights on, but she could see what she needed to see.

Puzzle's door was closed. The sigh of relief she let out felt so loud that she was surprised it didn't wake the Kellys. The kick-bolt was done properly. The door was bolted, but she *hadn't* put the clip in. Thank goodness she'd come! Puzzle was still munching hay, but she could easily have come up in the morning and found him gone. And quite apart from the horror of something happening to him, the very thought of what Declan would have to say – and Aidan, and Kitty, who probably wasn't her friend now anyway – was alarming.

She did the clip, looked in at Puzzle – a black hump at the back of the stable – and was speeding down the lane again within seconds.

The moon had disappeared behind a cloud and it was much darker. It felt like a proper midnight adventure. It was a shame, Lucy thought, that she wouldn't be able to tell anyone about it – her parents would be furious and say that pony was too distracting. The Kellys would be confirmed in their low opinion of her reliability. Maybe she could tell Erin – if Erin did get a pony. She could learn from Lucy's mistakes. She had asked Erin to come to Greenlands tomorrow – that was one thing she could feel good about – and Erin had said that, actually, she was going with her granda, but she'd be cheering for Rosevale.

The front wheel hit the pothole so hard that the jolt through her body hurt as much as the fall. She flew over the handlebars and landed with another jarring blow on the hard lane. Her left arm broke the fall, and the fall broke her left arm. Lucy knew – she felt it crack.

But it *couldn't* be broken. She scrambled up, whimpering, *Oh no, oh no.* Maybe it was just sprained. If she bandaged it up, tight, she would be able to ride tomorrow. She *had* to be OK. It wasn't just the money now. It was proving to Declan that she was reliable, proving to Aidan that she wasn't the spiteful coward he thought she was, proving Rosevale ...

Afterwards Lucy never remembered that agonising struggle home without wondering how she ever managed it. She knew she wouldn't be able to wheel her bike, so she pushed it into the hedge – the front wheel was buckled anyway – and, cradling her bad arm, feeling sicker with the pain every minute, limped home. She snuck in without her parents hearing, secreted some painkillers from the bathroom cabinet, and crept back to her cold bed. It took a long time to warm up again, and even longer to sleep, with the arm a throbbing deadweight across her chest.

Chapter 16

Lost Rider

EVERYBODY was nervous. Aidan understood that. Even though he was only the groom, he wasn't immune to the general tension. His dad was silent, Kitty twitchy – both of them were pale. Even his mum, making sandwiches he didn't think anyone would be able to eat, kept dropping the knife.

'Should I put in enough for Lucy?' she asked.

'*She'll* have money for the burger van,' Kitty said.

'I'll put some in anyway. Kitty, eat your breakfast or you won't have enough energy to ride.'

Kitty heaved a huge sigh and pushed egg around her plate.

Aidan escaped to the yard. It might be a special day, but there were still all the horses to be seen to – feeds and hay-nets to organise, beds to muck out, horses to be turned out in the paddocks. Only the team horses stayed in, with big breakfasts. Lucy had promised to be here early to groom Firefly, but it was after nine before she appeared, looking even worse than Aidan's dad and Kitty – greenish, in fact, and sort of hunched over.

Aidan said hello briefly. It might be The Day but he couldn't let go of last night's row that easily. He started grooming Ty. He could forgive Cam for not being here – she had her own yard to sort out and they were going to meet her at Greenlands.

'Dad says we're driving out of the yard at ten on the dot,' he reminded Lucy, because she was being *pathetic*, taking ages to hose Puzzle's leg, and letting him skip all over the place because she was trying to hold him and the hose in the same hand. She hadn't even started grooming Firefly. She needn't think he was going to do it – he had enough to do with Ty.

The yard was all bustle now, Aidan's dad and Kitty grooming their horses too, and his mum filling haynets for the lorry. Aidan ran a body brush over Ty's long body, which shone under the electric light like mahogany. It annoyed him this morning more than usual to see Lucy going into Firefly's stable. Maybe it was because today was The Day, or maybe it was because yesterday's wonderful ride had made Firefly feel properly his pony again. Anyway, this time tomorrow – no, less than that, by teatime today – Lucy would have to give him up.

'Lucy!' It was his dad's voice. 'What are you doing in there? Have you not got that pony ready yet?'

'Um, not quite.' Lucy's voice was unusually hesitant. 'Can somebody help me?'

Aidan sighed. Ty was ready, standing in his travelling rug, hooves shining with oil, looking like a racehorse ready to go to the Grand National. Aidan tied him up short, to make sure he didn't roll, and slipped into Firefly's stable next door.

Firefly wasn't even half groomed! A stable stain, wet and mucky, smeared one chestnut hock, and he had shavings in his tail. Lucy was brushing him feebly with one hand, not even using the curry comb to clean the body brush as she went.

'What are you doing?' Aidan cried. 'It's five to ten!'

Lucy turned. Her face was streaked with tears, and greyish green. 'I – I've done something to my arm,' she whispered. 'But don't tell your dad, please. I'll be OK. I can ride with one hand, if you just help me with this.'

'What have you done to your arm?'

'I – I don't know. I fell off my bike.' She bent over her arm and bit her lip so hard that it went as white as her face. 'Owww,' she moaned. She looked like she was going to be sick, and Aidan stood back a bit, but she said, 'I'll be OK.' She straightened up. 'If you groom him, I can ride him.'

Aidan didn't know much about first aid, not human first aid, but if ever he saw someone who wasn't fit to take charge of a pony – his pony – round a cross-country course, it was Lucy.

'You can't,' he said. 'Dad won't let you.'

'I have to. I can't let the team down.'

Aidan hadn't a clue what to do. But there was Firefly, waiting to be groomed, so he took the brush out of Lucy's hand. 'Sit down on the grooming box,' he said. 'Maybe you'll feel better in a minute.'

She sat down and leaned against the wall. Ten minutes later Firefly was groomed, the other horses were on the lorry, and Lucy clearly wasn't going to feel better in a minute or an hour or a day. And it looked as if Aidan would have to be the one to tell his dad.

Everybody stood round the stable doorway until his mum shooed Kitty away and told her to go and get Lucy's mum. Then she bent down beside Lucy and made her show her the arm. Once Aidan's mum took over, Lucy gave up all pretence at being OK and shook with sobs.

'Looks like it's broken,' his mum said. 'They'll have to take her to hospital.'

Then Lucy's mum appeared in her Merc, with Kitty in the passenger seat looking important, and Lucy was carted off to hospital, protesting that if they plastered up her arm tightly enough she might still be able to ride.

'She's brave enough, anyway,' Aidan's mum said, as they watched the big silver car drive down the lane.

'Stubborn,' his dad said. He sighed and ran his hand over his hair. 'Well, I suppose we should start unloading these horses.'

Kitty shrieked. 'You can't! It's the best three. They'll let us ride.'

Dad shook his head. 'Kitty – they won't. I checked the rules back when – before we got Cam.'

'But we have to enter!'

Aidan stood in the middle of them, holding Firefly's head-collar rope. The words were there, he only had to open his mouth and they would be out. But he couldn't. Even if his dad let him, he would be worse than useless.

He swallowed. Firefly stood beside him, solid and strong, glowing with fitness and good grooming, thinking he was going jumping, as he had done so many times before in his pre-Rosevale life.

He *can do it.* Firefly *can jump round that course. It's only* me ...

'I'll do it,' he said, his voice coming out scratchy so that he had to cough and say it again. 'I'll ride.'

Chapter 17

Frightened Pony

AIDAN sat beside his dad in the lorry cab. Kitty and Mum were in the back with all the mountains of stuff four horses and four riders needed. It was Mum who'd remembered about Lucy's team shirt, which luckily she'd left hanging from a nail in the tack-room.

'You don't have to do this,' his dad said for the millionth time.

'I do. It's fine.' Aidan swallowed, telling himself he did *not* feel sick, though his face in the rear-view mirror had the same greenish pallor as Lucy's had had.

His dad, never the most patient driver, swore as an overtaking car swerved in too tightly in front of the lorry. 'You're not ready. You haven't prepared. This team thing – it was a stupid idea from the start. I should have known. It's not the kind of thing we do.'

'Well, it is today,' Aidan said, surprised at how sturdy his voice sounded.

'But you mustn't take any risks, Aidan. Promise me. Only do the small jumps, and don't worry about anything you aren't happy about. As long as you're there to make up the numbers, that's all that matters.'

So he was only making up the numbers. And Olly and Josh were going to be there to see him make up the numbers. Every mistake, every failure of nerve – they'd be there to laugh and remember and tell everyone. Oh God, he really was going to be sick.

'If Kitty's jumping the small ones too,' he said, and this time his voice was thick and small, 'we aren't going to have much chance, are we?'

His dad hesitated. 'No,' he said in a low tone, as if he didn't want Kitty to hear this. 'Not of winning. Which is why I'm saying we can still turn back.'

It was so tempting! Like walking out of school yesterday. But he imagined telling Lucy that he hadn't even tried, that Rosevale couldn't manage to field a team at all.

'No.' Aidan's chin went up. 'You're the one always says we should be proud of the kind of yard we have. Folly and Firefly are both rescue horses. It's their chance to show what they can do.'

At least, he thought, watching the wipers swish their slow arc across the windscreen, *it is if I don't mess up.* He shivered.

Aidan had imagined the cross-country taking place right in front of the big house at Greenlands, which in his mind was a sort of mini Buckingham Palace. In fact the signs – CROSS-COUNTRY EVENT – directed them up a long tree-lined lane which led after half a mile to a huge bare hillside with a roped-off parking area at the bottom. Aidan counted at least twenty trailers and four lorries.

There was no sign of the big house, just some old stone outbuildings in the distance – stables perhaps – but the jumps marched menacingly up and down the hillside, flagged and huge and waiting. Aidan's heart swelled with fear. Behind him the horses, sensing from the lorry's slower movement that they had arrived, started to neigh.

'I'll get Firefly ready for you,' his mum offered, when they had all got out and stretched and looked around. There seemed to be thousands of people here, but no sign as yet of the two he didn't want to see.

Aidan shook his head. That was the easy bit, getting his pony tacked up, settling him down in the unfamiliar atmosphere – though, in fact, Firefly must have been used to places very like this in his jumping days. And he sensed that only by being with Firefly, reminding himself of the solid, kind reality of his pony, could he hope to calm down.

'First thing is to walk the course,' Cam said. 'The nags are OK where they are for now. Seaneen, maybe you'd stay and keep an eye on them?'

'Definitely,' Mum said. 'The last thing I want is to actually see close up what my kids and husband are mental enough to want to jump. I mean,' – she caught Dad's eye and changed tone abruptly –'they all *look* big to me but I can see they aren't. Not really.'

Trailing around with the rest of the team, huddling together away from all the other teams doing the same thing – only they all looked so professional – up the hill to the start and then down and round the figure-of-eight shape in which the jumps were laid out, Aidan tried to focus on what Cam was saying, but his head was so full of the terror of what he was about to do that he found it hard to make sense of the words.

You shouldn't be here. You won't be able to do it. And when you fail we'll be here to watch!

'It's a very straightforward course,' Cam was saying. 'No tricks. Especially the small jumps– there's only the water that might be a bit spooky. Keep your leg on here, Aidan. And you've got plenty of space, nothing too narrow. Good approaches. Now, it'll be muddy by the time you come to jump, so be careful. Try to make up time *between* the jumps, but don't take risks *at* them. Kitty – no heroics! Remember Midge is only twelve-two. You stick to the small jumps.'

'But if *I* do the small ones and *Aidan* does the small ones, we won't get enough –'

134

'Doesn't matter,' their dad cut in. 'Look, even with Lucy we didn't have much of a chance. But what we *can* do is jump round and show all those people what rescue horses can do, show them what Rosevale is all about. OK?'

Kitty looked mulish. 'I suppose.'

'Aidan?'

He nodded, speech being beyond him. OK for Cam to say it was a straightforward course. OK for his dad to say he didn't have to do it. They were both, he could see, eager to get round the jumps, wanting to test their horses and themselves. Kitty, too, half-drowned by her new team top, with all her curls forced into a tight plait, was weighing up the jumps with confident, knowledgeable eyes. Even if he'd had the weeks of Cam's schooling that the others had had, Aidan knew he would still have been the weakest link. But as it was, coming in at the last minute – who was he trying to kid?

While they tacked up, his mum went off and did all the official stuff, coming back from the registration stand with numbers for them. They were team eleven.

'Second last,' Dad said. 'It's not a very big field, really. It only looks like it because it's teams.'

Aidan recognised the names of some yards – riding schools and livery stables – but many of them were from other parts of the country, even a Donegal trekking centre with a very fancy green lorry. He both longed and dreaded to see the Sunnyside team, but when three of them did ride past, with the girls' hair all in plaits with oversized purple scrunchies on the ends, he was so busy helping Cam to pacify a rather overwhelmed Ty that he only had time to notice that they were all in purple with huge purple fluffy numnahs and velvet brow-bands.

There was no sign of Olly or Josh. Maybe they weren't really coming. The Sunnyside ponies looked nice enough – nothing special – but Jade's grey, frothing at the mouth and already curling with sweat on his unclipped parts, was clearly unhappy.

I might not be the best rider in the world, Aidan thought – 'Whoa, Ty, you're OK, it's just a loudspeaker' – *but at least I know better than to try to make my pony walk with its nose stuck to its chest.* Though probably Jade would jump round like a champion while he fell off at the first jump. He gentled Ty, rubbing his nose in the way that always calmed him, and held him for Cam to mount.

'Thanks,' she said. 'Didn't think he'd be this restless. Hope he doesn't think he's racing when he sees the course.' She spoke casually, but her face betrayed a trace of anxiety. 'Now, stop helping other people and go and get on! You'll be fine. Firefly is going really well and he can do it with his eyes closed. All you have to do is steer and hold on.' She gathered up Ty's reins. 'Don't want to keep him standing around fretting,' she called over his shoulder, riding away to find somewhere quiet to warm up.

Mounted, Aidan felt both better – because Firefly's back was a familiar place to be, and Firefly wasn't bothered by the hustle and noise – and worse, because now he knew this really was happening. Lucy's red and blue top felt new and strange. His dad and Kitty rode beside him to the flat bit of field which was being used as a warm-up arena, and they all walked, trotted and cantered on each rein.

'Now, you need to watch the first few rounds,' Declan said, 'just to get the idea of it.'

Although the course had grown in Aidan's mind to the proportions of Badminton, he had to admit, when he watched the first team, that it wasn't too bad. Unlike many cross-country courses, which disappear for ages into woodland and down the other sides of hills, the terrain here was such that you could see most of what went on from a couple of vantage points. The Rosevale team, with Aidan's mum now promoted to head groom and holding Alfie on a lead rope, were lucky enough to seize positions which let them see how most of the jumps were being jumped. A thin, oldish man with a straggle of gingery hair under a baseball cap was watching too, with the intensity of

137

someone who really likes horses. He smiled at them as they manoeuvred in beside the tape which marked the course.

'I've heard of yous,' he said in a strong Belfast accent like Aidan's parents. 'Yous do great work.'

Somehow the tiny exchange heartened Aidan and for the first time he was able to look at the course without feeling sick.

The jumps were arranged in a rough figure-of-eight, in three large fields. The hedges between the fields had, in places, been cut to make some of the jumps. In every case the small jump was right beside the big one. At every jump stood judges with score boards, to note which jump had been attempted. The scoring was eccentric – instead of the usual fault system, you gained ten points for clearing the big jump and five for the small. If you refused, you lost ten points. If more than one team finished on the same score, the fastest team won.

'It's a stupid system,' trumpeted a large girl on a heavyset warmblood who was waiting beside Aidan. She sat with her legs flung forward, her heels exaggeratedly down. Her purple numnah had SUNNYSIDE FARM embroidered on it in pink. Aidan looked round for Jade and co, but the other riders were from a different yard, wearing black and silver. 'Didn't I say, Angela, didn't I always say it was a stupid system?'

'Yeah,' said Angela. 'You did, Susie.'

'Sure, Dermie Doyle's never been to an event in his life. He's making it up as he goes along. He's just trying to buy his way in to the horsey set.'

'Somebody said he's a gypsy.'

'Everybody's making fun of him.'

Kitty's voice piped up shrilly from the other side of Aidan. 'Well, then the snobby gets shouldn't be here jumping over his land and trying to win his money. *I* think he must be a nice man.'

'Watch your language, Kitty,' Mum said. The old man in the baseball cap grinned at her.

'Watch the *course*,' Dad ordered. 'Cam – is that animal OK?'

'Bit hyper.' Cam sounded breathless and clearly had her hands full with a very het-up Ty, who was spooking at every noise and going into hysterics if a dog walked past – even Alfie. Aidan was grateful to be on Firefly, who took the sounds and sights in his stride. Folly was prancey and on edge too, but Aidan could see how his dad, with hands and legs and voice, reassured her that everything was OK.

The first team were very hesitant, stopping all over the place, and three out of the four went for the small jumps, so their score, when it was finally posted, was a feeble 105. The next team – the Donegal ones – were the opposite, very dashing and bold, and nobody went for the small jumps, so they got 290 marks in a combined time of five minutes fifty one seconds.

'We'll never beat that,' Kitty complained.

'We aren't trying to,' Dad reminded her. 'Just jump round safely.'

If Lucy were here, Aidan thought, he wouldn't be saying that. If Lucy were here there would be a chance, because Kitty's round wouldn't have to count. The thought depressed him so much he broke out of the watching line and walked Firefly about a bit on his own. There was no doubt about it, his pony was going well. Even walking, he was listening to Aidan. He remembered their gallop yesterday, the speed and lift and plunge of Firefly, fit and eager. It could be like that today, if he could forget there were people watching, forget the small matter of the ten jumps. *Just let them come at you*, was what Cam always said about jumps. All those training sessions at Cam's, when he had been the more or less unwilling groom, he had *listened*.

The fifth team was jumping now. It was all taking for ever, and yet it would soon be over, Aidan thought, smoothing the red strands of Firefly's mane. His hands sweated on the reins and he realised he wasn't wearing gloves. He rode back to the car park. A big purple lorry had squeezed in beside the scruffy Rosevale one, where there wasn't really enough space, and he had to manoeuvre Firefly carefully between them.

There was nobody much about. Everybody was watching the jumping. He could hear laughing and carrying on and the thud of running feet from the far side of the purple lorry, but he didn't pay it much attention until after he dismounted and loosened Firefly's girth. Then he heard the voice he'd been dreading.

'Ah, if it isn't My Little Ponyboy. This your nag? Ugly thing, isn't it? I was hoping to see the pink fluffy one.'

Don't react, Aidan told himself. *He can't do anything to you.* And surely even Olly wouldn't start a fight with someone who was actually holding a horse.

He led Firefly round to the back of the Rosevale lorry. He wanted to tie him up so he could go in for his gloves, but he didn't trust Olly, so instead he kept Firefly's reins over his arm while he rummaged in the tack box at the side of the lorry. He knew his own gloves weren't there but with luck he would find some old pair that would do. Hopefully *not* Kitty's old pink ones.

'Olly! Where are you?' Josh's voice came from the other side of the purple lorry. Well, it didn't matter what they did or said, he was just going to get his gloves and go. At least if they were messing round here it meant they weren't too interested in watching the actual jumping, so he might be able to make a fool of himself without them seeing. The voice came again

141

with a note of panic in it this time. 'Olly, c'mere, this thing's going mental!'

Ignoring them, Aidan delved through old tail bandages and lead ropes with broken clips. No gloves. Blast! If only there were someone *normal* around, he could get them to hold Firefly while he went in to fetch his own pair. Or if Olly and Josh would just go, he could tie his pony up safely.

A sudden high-pitched neigh from a frightened horse pierced the air, making Firefly start and twitch. Next minute, in a blinding flurry of mane, tail and hooves, a grey pony skidded round the side of the lorry. It took Aidan a second to realise that it had got its front leg through its reins. And two seconds to see that it was followed by a terrified, screaming, hopping Josh. 'It's broken my foot!' he yelled.

Aidan didn't have time to think. Praying that Firefly wouldn't panic, he tied him up roughly and approached the grey. It was snorting and plunging, eyes huge with panic, one leg hopping, caught up. It wouldn't take much for it to break a leg.

'Stop it, stop it,' blubbed Josh. 'It's going mental!'

'Shut up,' Aidan ordered in the quiet firm voice his dad always used in these situations. 'You're making things worse.' He reached his hand over to the terrified pony. 'Whoa,' he said. 'Steady the horse. Steady the good pony. It's OK.' With one hand he unbuckled the reins so they no longer formed a noose round the pony's front leg. The grey snorted and jumped, staggered on the captured leg, then, realising it was free, gave a huge shudder and relaxed.

'Good boy,' Aidan said, running a calming hand over the heaving shoulders.

Jade ran round the corner, in much the same state as her pony. 'What happened him? You were meant to be looking after him!' she screeched at her brother. She flung her arms round her pony, which backed away and tried to graze. Josh spluttered and sobbed.

Olly tried to bluster. 'He just went berserk for no reason. Wasn't our fault.'

'You *said* you'd look after him. You're pathetic! I wouldn't leave you with a toy horse.'

'He broke away. I couldn't hold him. He was *mental*,' Josh said. He wiped his eyes. 'Stupid animal! He nearly killed me. He stood on my foot. I bet it's broken.'

'He's a psycho,' Olly muttered. His face was even redder than before and Aidan wondered how he had ever been afraid of him.

The grey was grazing quietly now, only the curling, sweated coat and loose reins giving evidence of his recent panic.

Aidan heard his own voice, calm and somehow distant, say, 'He got his leg caught in his reins, but he's OK now.'

'Did you catch him?'

Aidan nodded. 'I didn't see what happened,' he said.

'*I* did.' Of all people, Erin from his class marched up. '*They* were teasing him.' She pointed at Olly and Josh. 'Trying to jump on him. And then *he*' – she pointed at Josh –'started crying because the pony stood on his foot. And he let go of his reins. If it hadn't been for Aidan, the pony'd have broken his leg.'

Olly and Josh looked foolish.

'You wait till I tell Mum, Josh,' Jade said. She turned to Aidan. 'Right. They have to thank you. *And* make friends.'

Aidan untied Firefly, mounted in one easy swing, and then walked him so close to Olly and Josh that he nearly went over the top of them and they backed away, their eyes big in their stupid faces. 'Don't bother,' he said loudly. 'I'm fussy who I make friends with.'

He rode off, feeling completely calm. How could he ever have let those snivelling, incompetent boys make him feel small? He was pretty sure they wouldn't bother him again, but even if they did, he knew he wouldn't let it get to him. So what if he liked horses? So what if they called him gay? He would keep the memory of them blubbing and freaking out somewhere very easy to reach.

But there was still the jumping. In all the excitement he had almost forgotten what they were actually here for, but as he rode back to his team, Firefly lively beneath him, glad to be on the go again, he knew that he might have won one big victory, but another battle was about to begin.

Chapter 18

The Final Score

EVERYONE agreed Aidan should jump last.

'It's only fair,' Cam said. 'See how the rest of us go and if we're all rubbish – well, there'll be no pressure. Gosh, Declan, have you no gloves? Here, take these.' She pulled off her gloves and handed them to Declan.

'You could even scratch if you wanted to,' Dad said. 'I mean, if we're so far out of the running.'

'I won't scratch,' Aidan said.

'That's 230 points for Sunnyside Stables, and now for one of our local teams, Rosevale,' intoned the impersonal voice over the PA.

It's real, Aidan thought. *It's actually going to happen now.*

Dad and Folly went first, Mum closing her eyes as they sailed over the first few jumps. 'I can't help it,' she said. 'When he was show-jumping it was bad enough, but this...'

She needn't have worried. After a slightly edgy start, with Folly overexcited and impetuous, she settled beautifully and took all the big jumps in her stride. Dad had to push hard through the water, and they all held their breath when she hesitated at the big hedge into the final field, but Dad gave the kind of kick he would have scolded Aidan and Kitty for, and they got through OK.

They galloped through the finish. One hundred points, in a time of one minute thirty one. It was the best round of the day.

'Well done!' they all called, as Folly slithered to a halt beside them.

Dad nodded, panting, his cheeks pink with galloping. 'Careful ... with the approach ... to the big spread in the first field,' he said. 'It's pretty churned up.'

'Next to go, Camilla Brooke for Rosevale, on Tyrone Top Cat.'

Ty took a while to settle into his round, stopping once at the water, but then waking up and realising that Cam meant business. He cleared all the rest with huge scope, and galloped home like the point-to-pointer he had been bred to be.

'Sorry about the stop,' Cam panted.

'Ninety points in a time of one minute fifty-eight.'

Kitty leaned over and whispered urgently to Aidan. 'We're one of the best so far. I *have* to go for the big jumps! It's our only chance. Dad and Cam won't be able to do anything about it.'

For a moment Aidan wanted to say *Yes! Go for it.* He had no doubt Kitty had the courage and the determination to try the bigger jumps. They weren't huge – she had tackled larger in the school – but these jumps were solid. If you hit them they didn't fall. And game little Midge was easily the smallest pony in the competition.

'Don't!' Aidan said. 'It's not worth it!'

'Well, are *you* going to?' Kitty flung back at him. And she cantered off to the start, both she and her pony looking so spirited and so tiny that she got an extra round of applause.

They cantered steadily to the easy first jump, a simple log. Right up until the last minute, Aidan was sure she would go for the small log, but she didn't: she headed straight for the big one. His breath caught in his throat as little Midge reached and stretched and made it.

Cam and his dad looked at each other. 'The wee –'

'She promised she wouldn't,' Aidan said unhappily.

Dad sounded annoyed but sort of proud too. 'I should have known.'

'But, Declan – she *can't* do all the big ones. Midge would never manage the big water! Or the downhill brush. She wouldn't be so stupid ... would she?'

Dad sighed. 'I don't know, Cam. I hope not.'

They were powerless, stuck at the top of the hill,

with a great view of what was happening, but unable to do anything to influence it. Aidan was so nervous for Midge – if *Kitty* wanted to break her neck it was her own lookout – that he forgot to feel scared when one of the helpers shouted over to him, 'OK, you, stand by.'

He cantered Firefly up to the start as if they were just going for a bit of a hack.

'Aidan!' He spun round in the saddle at the cry. Lucy, her arm in a huge plaster and sling, caught him up. 'How are we doing?' she demanded. 'I just got away this minute! And look, Erin's here.'

Erin grinned at him. 'I'm with my granda,' she said. 'He's mad on horses. That's who I take after.'

'Dad and Cam did well. Kitty's on now.'

Lucy and Erin fell into step beside him and together they looked down at Kitty, very faraway and small, Midge a toy pony cantering towards the third jump. He wondered if they had done the big one or the small one for number two.

'She's game anyway.' He recognised the accent of the old man again.

'Chip off the old block,' grunted another voice. 'Sure, her da could ride anything.'

Words, Aidan thought, *that are not going to be said about me.* Firefly pranced, ready to be off.

The third jump was a brush fence with a bit of a spread. Walking the course, Aidan had identified it

149

as one of the many he wasn't looking forward to. Its smaller companion was fairly innocuous, with hardly any spread. Surely Kitty wasn't going to –

But it seemed clear that she was. She chose her line, right into the big spread fence. Aidan, Lucy and Erin watched, silence heavy between them, as Midge stood back a little, then made a valiant leap and landed right in the middle of the jump.

'Ugh!' Erin and Lucy said together.

There was a tangle of pony and brush, with branches flying everywhere. And somewhere in the middle of it, the tiny doll – from this distance – that was Kitty.

Aidan groaned.

'I can't look,' Lucy yelped.

The tiny doll and the toy pony scrambled to their feet. Officials talked to Kitty. Aidan saw her nod, thought he heard her laugh, and then she was back on board. She trotted Midge round and then headed him for the smaller jump. He hesitated. 'Come on!' they heard, and next thing Kitty and Midge were safely over and galloping up the hill to the gap in the fence.

'Surely she'll do the wee ones now?' Aidan asked Lucy. 'She was told to.'

'She'll have time faults. It won't matter what she does now. Eejit! She shouldn't have been so reckless.' This, from Lucy!

He was about to ask why it wouldn't matter what she did now, when he realised. It was best three out of four. They had all assumed that *Aidan's* round wouldn't count. But now –

'Look,' Lucy said urgently. 'I know you didn't want to do this. And I know you don't think you've got what it takes. And I'm not trying to get you to take risks. But –'

'But you think I should try for the big fences.'

'Firefly can do it. Honestly, Aidan. These jumps – they're nothing to him. We did bigger ones at Cam's. He's a fantastic pony. I hate to say it, but he's even better than Puzzle.'

And Lucy was better than Aidan. If she had had both her arms she would have been about to start her round, and she certainly wouldn't have been going for the small jumps.

'OK, ready?' The helper gestured at him.

He stood at the start, feeling very alone, except for Firefly.

'Go!'

Aidan had always thought the worst thing would be the fact that people would be watching him. But once he got started, cantering towards the uphill log, which from the ground had looked easy – even to him – he had only the vaguest awareness of spectators. There was him, and there was Firefly, and it was just a matter of facing each jump as it came. Firefly's long red ears were pricked and he covered the ground easily. The log was behind them – from Firefly's back, the bigger one hadn't seemed much different from the little one, and now it was the gap into the next field. The bigger one looked huge, but it was brush, not solid timber – they had nothing to lose. *Firefly*, he kept reminding himself, *can do it.*

Firefly never felt like stopping. The unsure pony, needing his rider to tell him what to do, relying on his rider for confidence, had been replaced by this jumping machine. All thanks to Lucy. Aidan crouched over his pony's withers, galloping strongly uphill to the water.

But Firefly *wasn't* a machine, and when Aidan saw the water, how much deeper and longer the ten-point jump was, the pony checked, feeling his rider's uncertainty.

'Come on!' Aidan used his legs hard, steered firmly towards the middle of the big jump, grabbed a handful of mane and they were over.

That was the worst one, apart from the downhill. And if they wanted to, they could do the five-point downhill. Maybe it was better to be safe than sorry. After all, look what had happened to poor Kitty.

But as the downhill approached, he thought, *No! If I don't try, I'll never know.*

They seemed to be suspended in mid-air for ever, the landing looking a long way down. Once again he took a firm grip of mane – and they were over.

And now all they had to do was gallop like they had never galloped before. Crouched like a jockey, Aidan urged his pony on for the final stretch, but Firefly needed no encouragement. His ears laid flat back, he thrust himself forward in great pounding strides. Flags, people, dogs on leads, horseboxes like toys – all flashed past. He thought he saw Olly and Josh, open-mouthed, but they seemed like people from another world, nothing to do with him.

Galloping through the flags of the finish, they slithered to a breathless, triumphant stop.

The rest of the team crowded round.

'Was it clear? It looked clear, but we couldn't see the far side of the second field.'

'Don't tell me you did the big water!'

'I didn't think you could ride like that.'

'We did the ... the big *everything*.' Aidan felt the grin split his face. He slid down from his pony, ran up the stirrups and loosened the girth, using the chance to hide his face for a moment against Firefly's damp shoulder. There must have been other moments of triumph in his life, but right now, he couldn't think of anything to compare with this.

'Do you think we've won?' Lucy said what

everybody was thinking. 'Seaneen, haven't you written down all the scores?'

At that moment the loudspeaker crackled and the voice came over: 'That was another great round for Rosevale, one hundred points in one minute fifty-three.' So he had lost time at the water, with that stupid moment of indecision.

That makes a total for Rosevale of 290 points with a time of five minutes and 36 seconds. That's the team to beat! And now our final team, all the way from Fermanagh, it's the Shoreside Equestrian Club. And first to go for them is...'

They all turned to each other.

'You've done it!' said Erin, who seemed to have tagged on to them and to whom Kitty had taken a great shine because she said Midge was the cutest pony she had ever seen.

'No,' Kitty said, 'they've got it wrong. They've been making mistakes all day. Some of the others were clear.'

'No, they weren't, Kitty. Remember we thought that lot were clear but the grey stopped at the water, only we didn't see?'

'But were the Donegal ones not faster?'

Aidan's mum looked at her very scribbled-over list and screwed up her eyes at it. 'I *think* we're in the lead,' she said.

Kitty and Lucy and Erin started shrieking.

'Stop it!' Dad ordered. '*Shh*. Seaneen, let me look at that.'

There was a lot of counting and scrambling and checking and passing round of the list and arguing. Mum gave Dad a hug that went on for so long that Kitty complained, 'Mu-um!'

Aidan leant against Firefly, too tired suddenly to join in. Having started the day as groom, and graduated merely to make-weight, it was hard to adjust to suddenly being not just part of the team, but one of the ones who had made the best round. All the way round it had been about Firefly's ability and his own courage. Now the five thousand pounds had come back into the equation – and it was all too much.

The consensus seemed to be that they were, however unbelievably, in the lead.

'Now all we need is for this lot to do badly,' Lucy yelled gleefully. 'Let's hope they all fall off at the first jump.'

'Shh!' Cam warned her. 'You have a lot to learn about being sporting, young woman. And anyway, their first rider's just gone clear in a brilliant time.'

Lucy said nothing, but her mouth took on its familiar determined look, and Erin looked as if she was incanting some kind of falling-off spell under her breath.

It worked too. The second Shoreside rider, on a flashy palomino, after clearing the first jump, had a stop at the second, came round again with a ringing belt with her whip on the palomino's shining quarters, whereupon the horse stood straight up on its hind legs, deposited its rider in a heap and galloped off towards the car park. Lucy and Kitty looked at each other in glee. 'If that's their standard ...'

But it wasn't. Their third rider was clear and fast. The fourth had only one down.

'We're neck and neck!' Kitty shrieked. 'It'll depend on their times!'

'*Shh*,' Lucy and Aidan said at the same time.

'They'll tell us now,' Cam said.

The loudspeaker crackled and hissed.

Aidan chewed his nails. Lucy scratched her arm under the big blue plaster.

'And now the results.'

The Rosevale team all looked at each other.

'In first place, with 290 points in five minutes and 39 seconds is ... Shoreside!'

There was a ripple of clapping and some cheering.

'Second place, Rosevale.'

There was no money for second prize.

'Oh, well,' Cam said. 'We had a good day out. Now, for goodness' sake, clap and cheer and look like you mean it!'

'And we never expected to do this well,' added Dad.

'You were all brilliant.' Mum hugged Kitty, who burst into tears, and Aidan, who didn't, but could easily have done so if he had been nine and a girl.

'Well, that's that,' Dad said. 'Better get these horses home.'

They walked back to the car park, a silent, dispirited procession, apart from Cam who kept telling them how brilliant they'd been and reminding them that second place was way beyond what they had dreamed of.

If they had come tenth or fifth, Aidan thought, it wouldn't have mattered so much. It was being so close – just seconds away from victory – that was so infuriating. If he hadn't hesitated at the water ... if Ty hadn't spooked ... if Lucy hadn't broken her arm.

But at that thought he stopped, feeling the bulk of Firefly walking beside him across the pitted field, solid, warm, his own pony. Even for five thousand pounds he wouldn't have missed the chance to jump round that course on Firefly, to prove to himself that he could do it too. But at home at Rosevale, the roof still needed fixing, winter's chill was already breathing down their necks, and they still had too many ponies. Lucky Kitty, being young enough to cry about it. Though his mum, leading Midge for Kitty, said sharply, 'Stop it, Kitty. Do you want people to think you're a bad loser?'

Their lorry, parked beside the purple monster, looked shabbier than ever. There was hustle round the purple lorry, and a lot of talk and pointing as the Rosevale team approached. '*They* only came eighth,' Lucy said in what, for her, was a subtle whisper.

A tall thin woman with orangey lipstick and a very puffy body-warmer disentangled herself from the group and came over.

'I hear you saved Cody,' she said to Aidan. 'I'm Jade's mum.'

'Um, I just stopped him and undid his reins,' he said.

He hadn't told the rest of the team what had happened, so there were explanations and exclamations, helped out by a very enthusiastic Erin.

'He could have broken his leg,' Jade's mum said. 'We'd like to give you a reward for being so helpful.'

In a book, Aidan thought, she would write them a cheque for five thousand pounds, or at least send them enough bedding for the winter – because in a book her family would run a shavings emporium, or maybe a feed store. Free feed for life.

But it was real life, and he didn't want a stupid reward for just doing what anybody halfway sensible would have done.

'I don't need a reward,' he said.

He caught sight of Olly and Josh eating burgers. Yellow relish stuck to Josh's chin. Aidan remembered him hopping and crying. He smiled at Josh and knew Josh remembered it too. Then he went round the back of the lorry, tied Firefly up, untacked, rubbed him down, and put his fleece rug on, ready for the journey. The pony stood quietly, resting a hind leg.

'You were brilliant,' Aidan said, and because nobody was about, he put his arms round Firefly's neck and hugged him. 'Thank you.'

Firefly gave the little flutter with his nostrils that meant someone was coming, and Aidan pulled back. The old man in the baseball cap stood beside him. He put out a hand and stroked Firefly's neck. Firefly didn't flinch at the stranger's touch.

'Yous did very well, son,' the old man said. 'I thought for a while yous were going to win.'

'So did we,' Aidan admitted. 'Sorry,' he went on. 'I just need to put him into the lorry. It's too cold for him to be standing around.' He led Firefly up the ramp and tied him up with a hay-net. When he came out again the old man was still there, talking to his dad, who was holding Folly and Midge. Aidan stepped forward to take Midge and sort him out for the journey.

'I'm interested in your work,' the old man said. 'My grand-daughter's told me about yous. Are these rescue horses?'

'This one is.' Dad launched into the horrible tale of how he had found Folly starving in a barn with a dead mare and a dying foal, and of how it had taken years to teach her to trust people again. 'And Aidan's pony – the chestnut – maybe you saw him jump? Well, he was a grade A jumper until he had an injury, then they just got rid of him. He was going for meat.'

'All he needed was time,' Aidan put in. 'Dad, tell him about the black cob.'

Dad was never much of a talker but this was his pet subject, and as they got the horses ready – the old man stepped in to help, filling hay-nets from the bale Aidan carried out for him – he went on to describe some of the other horses Rosevale had helped.

The others appeared with Ty, and Aidan tried to introduce the old man, since he showed no signs of going.

'Are you here with a team?' Aidan asked politely, though every time he had seen the old man he had been alone. Probably lonely, and he obviously liked horses.

'No,' he said. He pushed his baseball cap back. 'I'm here with my grand-daughter.' He gestured at Erin, who grinned at him. 'And I suppose you'd call me a sponsor.'

'Sponsor?'

'Aye, I live here.' He held out his hand for Dad to shake. 'Dermot Doyle. Have yous time for a cup of tea up at the house?'

If Dad was as surprised as Aidan it didn't show in his voice. 'We ... well, we can't keep the horses standing round too long,' he said.

'Fair enough. Well, sure, we can have a wee chat now.' He sat down on an upturned water bucket. 'I've always loved horses,' he said. 'I grew up in the Markets – och, it's all knocked down now, but when I was a wee fella you'd still see the odd horse about. But the nearest I ever got to them was having a wee bet. I'd have loved to learn to ride but I worked on the roads all my days and I'd had five of a family to rear, and – sure, you know what it's like.' He looked at Erin. 'Maybe she'll get the chances I never had.'

Erin beamed. 'Granda's getting me a pony,' she said.

'Well, I got this lottery win,' Doyle went on. 'Yous'll have heard about it. And I always wanted a big house with land and horses about the place. I'm too old to learn to ride now –'

'I've taught older than you,' Cam said.

'But I'd just like to have the horses about me. I thought this competition might be the start of something – getting people in, letting them use Greenlands, but ... Och, I don't know. They're maybe not my type of people. I heard a few things...'

Not from us, thank God, thought Aidan.

'Anyway, I want to make a donation to your sanctuary. A regular one. And those old horses you

161

were talking about – the donkey and the shire horse and the wee foals – I've two hundred acres here. I'm not a farmer and I'm not going to try to be. I'm going to keep some fields for hay and I'm lending some out as allotments. But I wondered – would a couple of big meadows be any use to you? About thirty acres. I'll see to the fences. All you need to do is put the horses in and keep an eye on them. Well, I'd help out with that myself if you trusted me.'

'And they can keep my pony company when I get him!' Erin added.

'But you – you won ten million!' Kitty burst out. 'You could buy posh horses and get the best of lessons.'

'Cam's the best instructor,' put in Lucy. 'Erin, you should go to Cam. She's a bit bossy but she's brilliant. So should you, Mr Doyle.'

Doyle laughed. 'I don't think I'd have the nerve for it at my age,' he said. 'But I'd like to help horses that need it. So do you think we could have a deal?'

Chapter 19

Going Home

THE lorry came to a standstill in the darkening yard. Declan switched off the ignition, leaned back against the seat and let out a long sigh.

'Well, we did it,' he said. 'Not the way you planned, Lucy, but we did it.'

'Thirty extra acres,' gloated Lucy, 'and a big donation – I wonder how big?'

'I'm surprised you didn't ask him,' Cam said, and they all giggled.

'He heard me telling off those snobby girls,' Kitty said for about the tenth time. 'I think it was all down to me.'

'Erin saw Aidan helping that pony,' Seaneen said. 'So it might have been due to him.'

'It was a team effort.' Declan yawned. 'OK, we've got four cross-country stars to put to bed. Come on – we can't sit round here all night.'

Cradling her bad arm, Lucy couldn't do much to help, but she looked in at Puzzle and he came to meet her, blowing in her hair and biffing at her pockets for treats. She heard Aidan bringing Firefly into the stable next door.

'You were brilliant,' she said. 'I knew you could do it.'

This wasn't quite the truth. Nobody had been as surprised as she was to see him taking Firefly so boldly over all the big jumps.

Erin was going to have private lessons with Cam, and in the spring they were all going to help her find a pony. 'Why didn't you tell us who your granda was?' Lucy had asked her, but even before Erin had answered she knew the reason. She could just imagine how nicey-nicey Jade and Miranda would have been if they had known about the ten million pounds. They would be desperate to have Erin at Sunnyside now. Lucy grinned.

'It was you too. You made Firefly remember *he* could do it,' Aidan said.

They stood side by side, leaning on the adjoining half doors, watching their ponies eat, the electric light gleaming on their quilted rugs.

'Puzzle will be OK,' Aidan said. 'If he has to be turned out for a while he can go in Greenlands, with all the oldies. And you can ride Firefly if you want. Sometimes anyway.'

'Thanks.'

From the isolation stable there came a high-pitched neigh.

'Let's go and see Victor,' Aidan said.

'Victor?'

He shrugged. 'It feels like the right name to give a horse today.'

And they turned off the light, leaving their ponies pulling at the hay, and set off across the yard to persuade the newly christened Victor to be brave enough to eat carrots from their hands.

Because that was the wonderful thing about Rosevale, Lucy thought, watching the black cob inch across the stable to Aidan's outstretched, patient hand. There was always another horse to help.

THE END

Acknowledgments

AS always I am grateful to the friends and family who help me with all kinds of practical things, from pony-sitting to ironing, to give me time to write, and to travel to meet readers. Mummy, John, Anne, Patrick, Sharon, Caoimhe and Nicole – thank you!

Siobhán Parkinson and Elaina O'Neill at Little Island do the work of ten women; thanks to them for wanting this book in the first place and for being so fantastic to work with – again! And thanks to my agent Faith O'Grady, who continues to support me wisely and well.

A huge thanks to Claire Noble and all at www.ponymadbooklovers.co.uk for their enthusiastic response to my books. I hope you enjoy this addition to the stable!

Thanks to Rhona, Susanne, Elaine and Julie, who read and commented on the first draft; and especially to my youngest readers, Agnes and Saoirse. Lee Weatherly has been her usual wonderful helpful self, and her enthusiasm for my work means a great deal. Being granted a Major Award from the Arts Council of Northern Ireland will allow me to write fulltime next year, and I am very thankful for their continued support.